SIGNAL 33: FINDING ZOEY

A BROKEN HERO PROTECTOR ROMANCE

THE SIGNAL SERIES
BOOK 1

LC TAYLOR

Cover designed by Sweet 15 Designs
Editing by Alice I. Lunsford

LC Taylor
www.AuthorLCTaylor.com

Behind the Badge Press
www.BehindtheBadgePress.com

He saved me from the flames, only to set my soul on fire.

—*LC TAYLOR*

PROLOGUE

Finally.

After all the blood sweat and tears, Zoey was opening her business – Curvy Stitches. She'd secured the perfect location on Main street in downtown Cape Hallow. Her shop backed up to the water's edge, giving it a sassy vibe. Now, Zoey stood in the massive window overlooking the main road, as she dressed the mannequins.

Ever since she could remember, she loved making clothes. After two years at the community college, Zoey started turning her dream into a reality. It took almost five years working out of the house she shared with her mother, but here she was, a business owner. Her shop was more than she dreamed it could be. The lower floor consisted of a show-room for customers, with a small dressing room, and the back is where her magic came to life. Upstairs held a tiny studio apartment that allowed Zoey to finally move out of her mom's house. Not that she hated living with her mom, but at twenty-five, she was more than ready to live on her own.

A tap at the glass made her jump. Zoey glanced up to see a slender woman staring at her through the front of the store. Zoey smiled, stepping away from the mannequin, she unlocked the front door and tugged it open.

"Hi." Zoey smiled at the woman, "Can I help you with something?"

"Yeah – you can forget about opening your fucking store." She sneered, folding her arms across her chest.

"Excuse me?" Zoey gasped, confused that maybe she'd misunderstood the woman.

"You heard me. This shop is going to bring the rest of us down. Nobody wants a fat girl store here. It's embarrassing. I mean, look at you."

"You need to leave." Zoey pushed the door to close it, but the woman stuck her foot out, halting it from shutting.

"Seriously. Do yourself a favor and find a new location."

"Look, lady. I have no idea who you are… but I have no plans to move my shop because some deranged woman tells me I should. Now, please leave." Zoey pushed her out of the way and slammed the door, locking the woman out. Zoey watched as the woman stormed away. She was at a loss as to what just happened. Zoey grabbed her cell phone off the counter and called her mom.

"Hey, baby girl," she answered after the first ring.

"Hi, momma."

"So, what has my successful daughter calling me the day before opening?"

"Something weird just happened," Zoey took a breath, "This woman came by and all but threatened me to move my shop."

"What do you mean, move your shop? That's insane. Did she say why?"

"Just made some off-handed comment that a fat girl store would ruin the town's image. I slammed the door in her face."

"Good. Zoey, people are going to hate, that's just how life is – but you keep on moving forward. You have something wonderful to share with the real women of the world."

"Thanks, momma. That's why I called you. I knew you'd make me feel better."

"Now… how are opening day preparations coming?"

Zoey spent the next thirty minutes filling her in on the opening day plans. By the time Zoey finished talking to her mother, she'd managed to dress the windows and load all the stock onto the racks. After she was pleased with her work, Zoey turned off the lights and headed upstairs. Tomorrow was her grand opening, a day she'd been waiting for her whole life.

CHAPTER 1

Trigger Warning: This book contains stalking, violence, and
attempted murder.

THREE MONTHS. THAT'S HOW LONG SHE'D BEEN OPEN. ZOEY
was ecstatic that the business had been prosperous. The
women in Cape Hallow loved the fact there was a shop dedi-
cated to the more voluptuous gals. Growing up, a thicker girl
led Zoey to start her clothing line. Glancing around her shop,
Zoey couldn't help but smile. She was exactly where she
wanted to be in life at her age.

Of course, her mother insisted she needed a love life, but
Zoey was done trying to find love. The last man she'd dated
wanted to change her – saying if she only worked out, she'd
be a better woman. He turned out to be a control freak and
suffocating, but not in a good way. Breaking it off had been
hard because he wouldn't take no for an answer. But after
relentless arguments and threats to involve the police, he'd
finally left her alone.

After that, she decided to give everything to her career rather than try and change for a man. She was happy with her curves. Zoey was tall for a woman, standing at five foot ten.

And skinny, she was not.

She had a curvy body that left little to a man's imagination. Her clothes intentionally highlighted those aspects of curvy girls. Zoey had long decided to flaunt her stuff in fitting attire rather than hide under baggy clothes. She figured if a man wanted a curvy girl, he'd love her and her curves. If not, oh well.

She decided she didn't need a man to be happy.

Glancing around the closed shop, Zoey grabbed the mail piling up on her desk. It was time to sift through the bills and pay them. This was the not-so-fun part of the job. Thankfully, she made enough to pay them and earn a salary. Sifting through the envelopes, she found a peculiar one at the bottom. It was addressed to her, not the business. Tearing open the seal, she unfolded the paper. Sucking in a breath, she was stunned to read the note.

> YOU HAVE WHAT I WANT... I'LL GET WHAT'S
> MINE SOON ENOUGH.

There was no signature on the note, and when she turned the envelope over, she realized there was no return address. Zoey decided this was just another hater and tossed the ridiculous letter in her drawer. It wasn't the first time she'd gotten hate mail. Hell, since opening, Zoey had her share of pissed-off Barbie dolls. She couldn't understand why they hated her presence so much. There was plenty of business that catered to their body style. Her shop attracted curvy women like her —

so listening to their stupid complaints and threats didn't mean anything.

Zoey wrapped up what she was doing and decided to grab a late dinner. Everything was close by, so walking to the diner around the corner took her no time. Everyone, well, mostly everyone, treated her kindly. The diner's owner, Charles, greeted her with his usual wave and smile. He was an older man who started the restaurant in his early twenties. Now, years later, it was the hot spot in Cape Hallow. Zoey pulled out her phone and pulled up the latest romance. She often enjoyed reading while she ate alone.

"When are you going to make some friends, pretty lady?" Charles's raspy voice drew her from her book.

"Charles," she smiled at the old man, "I don't have time for friends. My business keeps me busy enough."

"Pshhh," he grunted, "Everyone needs friends, my lady. You're no exception. What happened to all those girls you hung around in high school?"

"They grew up and moved away. I was the only one that stayed here – you know that."

"And what about a man?"

"What about a man? You know I'm not what the men around here want."

"What does that mean? Zoey – you're gorgeous. Any man who doesn't want a woman with curves is a fool."

"Yeah – well, finding a man like that is about as possible as finding a unicorn in the woods."

Charles laughed hard as the chime to the door interrupted their conversation. Charles turned to greet the newcomer. Over his shoulder, he said, "Well, back to work for me. Seriously, Zoey – you deserve some fun."

Zoey couldn't stop staring at the man placing an order at the counter. He was tall – taller than her anyway. And his arms were massive. She couldn't see the rest of his body beneath the clothes he wore, but the dark blue t-shirt hugged his back like it was made of silicone. She couldn't stop staring - it was like her eyes were magnets, and he was made of metal. Charles cocked an eyebrow at her from behind the counter, making her blush. Rolling her eyes at him, she didn't realize the stranger had turned around. She caught his gaze, feeling heat wrap around her body as she smiled at him. That's when Zoey noticed his shirt's Cape Hallow Fire Department logo. Holy hell, he was a fireman… a hot one at that.

Zoey looked back down at her phone, embarrassed to be caught staring at him. She didn't want him to think she was some creepy girl ogling him. Zoey didn't glance up until she heard the chime of the door. Charles winked at her, "He works over at station three on the engine. Nice fella."

"And you're telling me this why?"

"Woman, I saw the way you were looking at him. You couldn't go wrong with a guy like that."

"A guy that looks like that would *definitely* not be looking at a girl like me."

"Zoey… you've got to stop putting yourself down. Not every idiot wants a girl that could blow away with the next big hurricane."

"They don't want a big girl like me, either. Been there, done that. Every guy I've dated wants to help me get healthy," Zoey stood up, tossing a few bills on the table for a tip, "as if I'm unhealthy the way I am. See you later, Charles – tell the missus I said hello." Zoey waved at Charles as she exited the diner, glad she lived close. The weather here was always warm, being a beach town, and close to the ocean, even late in the year, the temperature stayed enjoyable. Tonight was no different.

Zoey's phone vibrated in her bag. Digging it out, she smiled, seeing her mother was calling her.

"Hi, mom."

"Zoey. I wanted to see if you wanted to go to the street festival with me tomorrow. It starts at ten in the morning. I don't want to go alone."

"Of course, I'll go with you. I want to check it out and see if I want to participate next year as a vendor."

"Great!" Her mom squealed, "I'll meet you at your place tomorrow morning around nine-thirty since it's going to be down main street anyway."

"Ok. See you then, Mom."

Zoey tossed her phone back into her bag and fished out her keys. As she approached the front door to her shop, she was shocked to see the glass panel shattered. Someone had kicked out the intricate glass panel that ran down the center of the oak door.

"What the fuck?"

She dug her phone out again and turned on the flashlight. The bottom glass panel of the entrance was a crumpled mess on the interior floor. It also looked like there was damage to the frame, making Zoey think it had been a break-in. Stepping away from the store, she dialed 911.

It didn't take long for the cops to show up. After inspecting the premises, they determined it looked more like vandalism as nothing had been taken from inside. The officer was concerned with structural damage and requested the fire department to assess the building. They didn't want to risk her safety.

Zoey sighed, knowing her peaceful night had been ruined. She sat on the curb, waiting for the fire department to arrive. Zoey prayed they weren't going to ruin her night more by telling her the building's structural integrity had been compromised.

CHAPTER 2

Dawson had just finished his food when the non-emergency call came in. The police department requested them on-scene to a vandalism to check that there wasn't any structural damage to the building. He recognized the place right away – Curvy Stitches. It was a little boutique that catered to thicker women… women he preferred.

Hopping in the truck beside Oren, he smiled, "I wonder who would vandalize Curvy Stitches…"

"Right? It seems stupid to damage the place, but the officers on the scene insist it wasn't a break-in. Just property damage."

They pulled the truck alongside the curb; Dawson immediately noticed the broken door.

"Fuck. They did a number on the front door and bent the hell out of the frame." He tilted his head, tracing the frame from top to bottom with his eyes. "Let's find the owner and check it out."

Dawson and Oren hopped out, meeting Kristof and the lieutenant at the back of the truck. The four of them made up the crew on engine three. "I'll go assess the entry, Dawson, find the owner, and see if she has something we can use to cover the hole."

"Yes, sir," Dawson turned, searching the area for the owner. He spotted a woman sitting on the curb down from the truck. Her head was bent over with her forehead resting in her empty palm, her phone pressed to her ear, talking to someone.

"Yeah, mom. No… I'm not coming to your house. The cops said it was safe to stay in my apartment. Mom. Seriously. No – look…" She sighed into the phone, "I gotta go. The fire department is here. Yeah… fine. I'll call you then."

He watched as she shoved her phone in her bag and pressed the heels of her hands to her eyes.

"Ma'am." Zoey jumped at his voice, unaware someone had been standing near her.

"Fuck. You scared the shit out of me." She glanced up at the man standing beside her.

"Sorry – are you the owner?"

"Yep," She stood, sticking her hand out to shake his, "Zoey Horton. So, what's the verdict?"

Dawson took her hand in his, aware of the heat from her touch. Releasing her grasp, he stepped back, waving his free arm toward the storefront. Zoey realized he was the man from the diner, "Wait – you were in the diner earlier."

"What? Oh yeah. I was getting the crew dinner. Did this happen while you were there?"

"Seems that way… Anyway. What did you find? Was there structural damage done?"

"Let's step over here. My lieutenant is inspecting it now. Do you have anything we can use to cover the hole?"

"Um… yeah – if I can get inside, I have some plywood left-over from the renovations. It's in the back."

Dawson led Zoey towards the entrance, "What'd you find, LT?"

"No structural damage, but you'll need a new frame and door. We can cover it up for you if you have some wood. I'll go grab some tools." Zoey nodded, glancing between the two men.

"Alright, let's go get that plywood."

Dawson placed his hand on the small of her back, leading her inside. Zoey couldn't help the shiver his touch elicited.

"You alright?" Dawson furrowed his brows at her.

"Yeah – sorry, just tired and pissed. Here we go," Zoey pulled open the storage closet and tugged out a relatively large piece of plywood. Dawson reached to grab it from her, but Zoey stopped him, "I can get it."

"Nonsense. Let me take it."

"I'm not some small woman if you hadn't noticed."

Dawson appraised her body, his eyes soaking in the length of her tall, curvy frame. "Oh, I noticed. But let me do my job."

She pushed past him, stopping to gape at the giant hole that was once her front door. "I don't understand why anyone would do this."

"Probably just some stupid kids. We'll get it all sealed up for you tonight. I can give you the name of a contractor to call in the morning."

"Nah, I did all the renovations myself, so I can certainly fix a damn door."

Dawson smiled, utterly stunned at the woman standing in front of him. "Well, if you need some help, let me know. I could do the heavy lifting." He winked at her as he began to fasten the plywood to the wooden frame.

"Thanks, but like I said – big girl." She pointed at herself, "I can manage. This is a curvy woman's store, after all."

Dawson ignored her as he wrapped up the temporary fix. Stowing the tools in the truck, he watched his crew climb in the cab, "Well, if you need anything else, feel free to call again."

"Thanks for the help, um…" Zoey tilted her head, "I didn't get your name."

As Dawson climbed into the rig, "Dawson Ford. Oh, and Zoey," He smiled, "You're not a big girl – you're beautiful."

He tugged the door shut, leaving Zoey with her mouth agape as the truck pulled off. Men like that never spoke to her in that way – she didn't know what to make of his ballsy comment. Once the truck was out of sight, she turned and headed inside. One of the firemen had given her a chain and lock to secure the door shut until it could be repaired. Once she was confident it was secure, she headed upstairs to her apartment. After calling her mom and filling her in on the events, she collapsed in her bed, exhausted. After the festival, she'd be buying a new door and installing it tomorrow.

CHAPTER 3

Things seemed to settle down over the next couple of days. Zoey had spent the afternoon with her mom enjoying the festival – it was a welcome break from the headache of her damaged storefront. She'd wound up hiring a contractor to come out and replace the broken door while she was out with her mom. She was pleased with the replacement - but still pissed she had to have it done.

Zoey stood behind the counter as several ladies perused the racks of clothes. Even though she was no closer to figuring out who had smashed in the door, she couldn't help but smile that the business hadn't been affected by closing for a few days. As Zoey rang up the last customer, the bell dinged, indicating someone had entered the store.

"Sorry, but I'm closing up for the day." Glancing toward the stranger, she sucked in a breath, "What are you doing here?"

"Hello to you, too." Dawson smiled at Zoey, "I wanted to stop by and see how the store was doing."

"Oh. It's great, thanks."

"I like the new door. Any leads on who did the damage?"

"Nope. They said it was probably some kids messing around. Anyway, I need to close up." Zoey stood still, waiting for him to leave.

"Oh," Dawson glanced at her, then toward the door, "Um… look," He rubbed his hand over his face, "I didn't just come to check on the store. I wanted to see if you'd grab a bite to eat with me."

"You want me to eat with you? Like a date?" Zoey didn't know what kind of sick joke he was playing, "You can't be serious."

"Why wouldn't I be serious?"

"Look, Dawson – I appreciate you being kind, but you don't have to ask me out on a date."

"I wasn't asking you on a date, to be kind. I wanted to get to know you, Zoey."

Zoey didn't know how to respond. Men who looked like Dawson did not hit on her – so why him?

"I don't think that's a good idea."

"Why not? If it makes you feel better, we could go as two people getting to know each other as friends."

Zoey pondered his request. She could be friends with him, but nothing more. She wasn't about to let her heart get crushed by someone again.

"Friends?"

"Yeah… friends. So, what do you say? Dinner?"

"I need to lock up first." Zoey moved around, cashing out the register and locking it in the safe. She cut off all the lights and headed out the front, Dawson following her. Once she locked the front door, "So where to?"

"How does Pizza sound?"

"Perfect." Zoey followed Dawson as he led the way to the pizza parlor just down from her shop.

"Hey, Zoey." Aby, the restaurant owner, greeted her, "Sit wherever you like."

Zoey smiled at her and guided Dawson to a booth in the back. Dawson slid into the booth across from her, "This place is nice."

"Yeah – it's been here forever. Aby has been the owner for as long as I can remember."

"Did you grow up here?"

"Yeah. Born and raised here. What about you? Where are you from?"

"From about four hours north of here. I was in the military for the first half of my adult life, then got out and came here."

"Wow. What did you do in the military?"

"Firefighter."

"Oh. I guess that was a stupid question. How long were you in?"

"Joined right out of high school. Did four tours overseas before getting out – so fourteen years."

"Wow. You don't look old enough to have done fourteen years. That makes you, what, thirty-two?"

"Yep – that an issue?"

"What – no. I'm just surprised, is all."

"What about you? How long have you been a business owner?"

"Sorry to interrupt, but can I get you two something to drink?" Aby smiled.

"How about a pitcher of beer? You don't mind beer, do you?" Zoey cocked her eyebrow, smiling at Dawson.

"Funny. I didn't take you for a beer drinker – beer's fine."

"Great – and can we get a large pie, meat-eaters? If that's ok with you." Zoey smiled again.

"I think I might love you." Dawson chuckled, "It's exactly what I would have ordered."

The waitress smiled, Dawson's comment making Zoey blush.

"Great – I'll be out with your drinks in a minute."

Dawson watched the waitress walk away, "So... back to our conversation. How long have you owned Curvy Stitches?"

"Oh - it's been mine since opening day three months ago. I've always loved making clothes, so after two years at community college, I decided I wanted to have my own place. I lived with my mom for the last five years, saving up and getting my online presence built up. Now – here I am at twenty-five, a business owner."

"That's fucking amazing, you should be proud. What about your mom? She still in the area?"

"Yes. We talk every night, and I make sure to see her as often as I can. It's been just her and me for as long as I can remember. My dad died when I was seven from cancer."

"Sorry to hear that."

Zoey noticed Dawson tense up at the mention of her dad, so she quickly changed the subject to something else. They fell into easy conversation as they ate. Zoey couldn't help but smile. Dawson was not what she expected. He was kind, genuine, and fun to be around.

"So – how was this non-date?" Dawson pushed the door open, following Zoey out onto the street.

"Probably one of the best non-dates I've ever had. Thanks for this. It's the most fun I've had in quite some time."

"Good – does that mean we can do this non-date thing again?"

Zoey blushed, "Maybe."

Dawson walked beside her, "Can I walk you upstairs and make sure you get inside safely?"

"Um… I think I can manage the steps."

"Fine… friends?" Dawson stuck his hand out.

Zoey eyed his palm, slowly placing her palm in his, "Friends."

"See you around, Zoey."

"See you around, Dawson. Wait," she pulled her phone out, "let me text you my number – since we're friends."

Dawson smiled as he rattled off his number.

"There, now you have my number."

Dawson grinned, "Alright, friend. I'll call you to schedule another non-date soon."

Zoey watched him jog around the side of the building. She unlocked her door and stepped inside. As she was locking the door, her phone beeped. Glancing at the screen, she couldn't stop the smile that burst from her lips. The unknown number had to be Dawson.

Unknown: Had a great time tonight.

She replied immediately,

Zoey: Same here… it was great getting to know you.

Zoey stored his number on her phone, her cheeks hurting from the permanent grin she had.

Dawson: Good night, beautiful.

Zoey: You too.

Zoey plugged her phone in before stripping down to her underwear. Slipping into the crisp sheets, her mind strayed to the hot fireman she was calling a friend. She didn't want the mess of dating, but something about Dawson caused her body to tingle, telling her she was going to have a hard time with just being his friend.

CHAPTER 4

DAWSON STRETCHED OUT ON THE COUCH IN THE COMMON room, he couldn't stop thinking about Zoey. She was more than he could ever want in a woman – and although something was holding her back, he planned on showing her just how much he wanted her more than as a friend.

"Dawson, what the hell has you so dreamy eyed?" Kristof kicked his boot and plopped down next to him.

"What the fuck are you talking about?" Dawson swatted at him.

"You got this fucked up grin on your face…"

"No. I don't. You're an idiot. I'm just tired."

"Right. I saw Curvy Stitches is all fixed up. Still don't get why it was targeted."

"Yeah, me either. The owner seems too nice to have anyone looking to harm her."

"Yeah – Zoey was the quiet girl in school. Kind of a loner."

"Oh, did you know her well?"

"Nah, not really. I moved here my senior year, and Zoey wasn't really part of the popular crowd. I was on the football team and ran with that crew. She's a big girl – was then too."

"Big girl?" Dawson's hackles rose, "She's gorgeous and curvy – not big."

"Woah... calm down, boy. I'm just saying she didn't fit in because she was curvy back then."

"Because she was curvy? That's really fucked up, Kristof." Dawson shook his head, "Zoey is a real woman."

"Someone has a crush." Kristof grinned.

"Shut up." Dawson stood and headed upstairs, "I'm going to catch some sleep."

Once in his room, he couldn't resist texting Zoey. He hadn't seen her since their non-date a couple of days ago and had only traded a few simple text messages since then.

Dawson: How's business?

He smiled at her immediate response.

Zoey: Busy today... how's work for you?

He fired a quick response.

Dawson: Slow. A few medical calls so far.

Zoey: Interesting…

Dawson decided to ask for another non-date

Dawson: How about another non-date
Saturday?

Zoey: I don't close until 8. How about dinner
at my place?

He was glad she couldn't see his face when he responded.

Dawson: Is that too date-date for you?

Zoey: Nah – we'll eat take out and watch
bad movies…

Dawson: Great, I'll bring the takeout – you
pick the movies.

The alarm went off, signaling it was time to work.

Dawson: Gotta go – alarm call. Text you
tomorrow.

Zoey: K Be safe…

Dawson slipped his phone into his pocket and rushed down the steps. Leaping onto the truck, he smiled, knowing he was going to spend more time with the feisty redhead who had no clue how beautiful she was.

CHAPTER 5

Zoey couldn't believe what she was seeing. Another threatening note. This one was like the other – making accusations that she had something that was theirs. She couldn't understand why someone believed she had something that belonged to them. Crumbling up the paper, she tossed it into the trash can and stood. Dawson was due in a little while, so she wanted to finish closing to be ready. Walking to the front door, she bolted the lock in place and turned off the open sign. Turning off all the lights, Zoey hurried to the back and up the stairs that led to her loft apartment.

Dashing around, she tidied up, stowing her dirty clothes in the closet just as her phone beeped.

Dawson: Outside. How do I get in?

Zoey: I left the back door open. Go in and
up the stairs.

Zoey heard his footsteps ascending the stairwell, smiling, she pulled open the door to find Dawson standing on the other side. He was dressed in a pair of loose jeans and a snug t-shirt that highlighted every muscle hidden beneath the fabric.

"Hi. Welcome." Zoey stepped aside and waved him in. She pointed to the bags he was holding and shut the door, "That smells good."

"Picked up Thai food. Hope that's ok with you."

"I'll eat anything – as you can tell." She waved her hand down her body.

Dawson reached out and grabbed her hand, "Hey, don't do that. You are a beautiful woman."

Zoey pulled her hand free, "Thanks, but I'm not blind nor dumb. I've spent my whole existence knowing I wasn't like the other girls – and I am ok with that. I own my curves. Hell, it's why I started my business. Curvy women deserve to look good, too."

"Well, you do." Dawson set the bags down on her counter and turned, "look good."

Zoey stared into his eyes, their gazes never breaking. Zoey swallowed, "You hungry?"

Dawson never broke his gaze, "Famished."

Zoey's heart thundered in her ears. The way he was looking at her, she was positive he wasn't talking about food. She gulped, "I'll grab plates."

Breaking eye contact, Zoey pushed passed him to grab the paper plates, but Dawson reached out and grabbed her arm. "Zoey," his voice sounded strained.

"Yeah?" Zoey kept her head turned away from him, afraid to look at his face.

Dawson pulled her towards him, his fingers going to her chin to tilt her face to his. He ran his thumb down her cheek, slipping his hand behind her head, tangling his fingers into her hair. Dawson looked at her lips, allowing her to pull away. When she didn't, he dragged her mouth to his, fitting his lips over hers.

The heat that Zoey felt caused her to moan, her body instinctively pressing into his. Her arms wound around his neck as his free hand traced down her side and fit against her bottom. She could feel his arousal pressing into her stomach, causing her to gasp. He pulled back, resting his forehead against hers.

"I'm sorry. I know that isn't part of our non-date rules. But I couldn't go another minute without kissing you. Zoey – I like you. And not just as a friend. But if this is too much, I'll leave."

Zoey closed her eyes, her body still pressed against his. She didn't know what she wanted long-term, but without a doubt, Zoey knew she wanted him right now.

She cupped his cheek, "Shut up and kiss me again."

Dawson didn't hesitate. He pressed his lips to hers again. This time, Dawson cupped her bottom with both hands and hoisted her up onto the counter. Pressing himself between her legs, he ground his erection into her groin. Zoey wrapped her legs around his back, pulling him into her harder.

Dawson slipped his hands beneath her shirt, cupping the lacy bra. Zoey moaned, leaning her head back as Dawson nibbled his way down her neck. He snatched the thin blouse she was wearing and pulled it over her head.

"Fuck, you're beautiful." Dawson leaned down and pulled the lacy fabric to the side, and sucked her pert nipple into his mouth. Zoey pawed at his shirt, trying to get it off. Dawson laughed, releasing the pink flesh from his lips, and tore his t-shirt off.

Zoey bit her lip, running her hands along the ripped muscles lining his chest. "I want you."

"Are you sure?"

"Yes."

She squealed when Dawson lifted her off the counter and carried her towards the bed.

CHAPTER 6

Zoey's lips pressed against his as Dawson tugged her pants off, stripping her down to her panties. Zoey propped herself up on her elbows, watching Dawson.

"You have too many clothes." She toed at his jeans. Giggling as Dawson stood and shucked his pants, Zoey suddenly sucked in a breath when Dawson stood before her naked. His cock was the most beautiful dick she'd ever seen. It was thick and long, "Holy shit." Zoey wasn't a virgin, but her sexual experiences were limited, and never had she been with anyone as large as Dawson. "I don't think you're going to fit."

"It'll fit. But first, I'm going to make you cum." He kneeled, tugging her legs so her butt rested on the edge. He draped her legs over his shoulders and nipped at her thighs as he licked his way towards her center. Zoey let out a moan as Dawson licked her from end to end, his lips latching on to her sensitive bud. Zoey screamed out, the sensation almost too much. Dawson's tongue dove in and out of her folds, lapping up her juices. He slipped in a finger, curving it to the spot that pushed her over the edge.

Zoey felt her stomach tighten. The electric tingles of her orgasm burst free, spilling from her lips as she screamed out Dawson's name.

Dawson grinned, kissing his way up her body, swirling his tongue around her nipple before capturing her mouth with his. He laced his fingers with hers, pressing her hands above her head as he wedged his body between her legs. Dawson nipped her lip as he thrust inside her slowly.

"Fuck…" He hissed, pausing to give her time to adjust, "You're so fucking tight."

"I need you to move…please." Zoey bucked against him, her legs wrapping tightly around his ass, drawing him inside her.

Dawson eased out, slamming back in, finding a rhythm that matched her screams. He was like a man in need – frenzied by her touch.

Zoey could feel the passion building, her body taut with need. Dawson knew precisely where and how to work her. She tensed, screaming out his name as her orgasm rippled out of her center. Dawson stiffened as he lost control, spilling his seed deep within her walls.

"Holy shit." He rolled off her, his semi-hard cock slipping out. "That was…" he sighed.

"Amazing." Zoey finished for him as he tugged her against his side.

"Fuck," Dawson rolled to look at her, "I forgot a condom."

Zoey's eyes grew round, "Oh…" she looked away, "It'll be ok."

"I'm sorry. I guess I got caught up and dropped the ball."

"Seriously. It's ok. I'm on the pill, and I haven't been with anyone in a long time. I'm clean." Zoey traced her finger in circles on his chest.

"Me too. Clean, I mean. I got tested when I started with the department, and I haven't been with anyone since moving here."

"Are you hungry?"

Dawson's stomach grumbled on cue, "I could eat."

Zoey shifted out of his arms and stood. Grabbing a towel, Zoey cleaned herself off. She grabbed his t-shirt and slipped it over her head. Even though she was curvy, his shirt was oversized on her. Dawson pulled on his boxers and followed her to the counter. He sat on the stool, watching Zoey heat their food in the microwave.

"So…" Zoey smiled as she scooped food onto plates, "I guess this was not a non-date."

Dawson tugged her hand into his, "Zoey – I think we both know there is no way we can be friends. I like you way too much."

Zoey nodded, "I just…" she turned, grabbing a bottle of water from the fridge, "Why me, Dawson? Don't get me wrong. I like you – a lot. But you could have anyone you want."

Dawson stood from the stool and wrapped his arms around her, "I like you, Zoey. I thought you could tell." He pressed his growing erection into her backside. "Will you give me a chance?"

Zoey turned in his arms. Eyeing him, she stood on her tiptoes and pressed her lips to his, "Yes," she turned, "now let's eat. I worked up an appetite."

Dawson helped Zoey carry the plates to the couch. Zoey propped her feet in Dawson's lap and turned on a rom-com. They ate silently, pretending to watch the movie. When Zoey was done, she set her plate on the table. Dawson set his empty dish next to hers. He grinned at Zoey as he sat back against the couch.

He slid his hand up her bare leg, slipping his hand beneath the edge of her shirt towards her center. Zoey watched him, spreading her legs to allow him easier access. Dawson leaned forward, pushing his finger into her core as he captured her lips in a scorching kiss. He pumped his digit into her wet center, causing her to moan. Zoey pressed his back against the couch and straddled him. Their mouths tangled, tongues dancing in a sensual make-out session.

Zoey lifted, slipping her hand beneath the smooth fabric of his boxer briefs, and freed his cock. Spearing herself on his rod, Zoey moaned as she began to move. Dawson gripped her hips, thrusting himself inside her as she rocked against him. Her movements became hurried as she raced towards her release. Gripping his shoulders, Zoey screamed out as she squirted all over his dick. Dawson moaned, his balls tightening as he shot his load into her walls.

"FUCK." He grunted, spearing her from below.

Zoey collapsed against him, "That was some awesome dessert."

She slowly stood, slipping off his lap, and grabbed a handful of napkins. She wiped the sticky mess from her legs and tossed them into the trashcan.

Glancing at the clock, "Shit… I have to be up in six hours to open the store."

Dawson realized it was nearly midnight, "I should go."

Standing, he grabbed his pants off the floor and pulled them on. Zoey went to pull off his shirt, but Dawson stopped her.

"Keep it. It looks good on you." He leaned in and pressed a kiss to her forehead. "How about a real date this week?"

"I'd like that. When are you on shift again?"

"Monday. Off Tuesday and Wednesday."

"I close early on Wednesday. How about dinner at six?"

"I'll pick you up."

"Ok. Dawson," Zoey leaned against the open door, "I had a good time tonight."

He leaned in, capturing her lips in a kiss, "Me too. Get some sleep."

Zoey watched him walk down her steps and disappear out the door. She hadn't felt this happy in a long time.

CHAPTER 7

Dawson couldn't get rid of the smile on his face. He liked Zoey so much that she filled his thoughts regularly. They'd shared a few conversations on the phone since their time Saturday, but his body craved more.

"Dawson… how was your weekend?" Davis, the EMT on shift, pulled out a chair and sat next to him.

"It was good."

"Do anything fun?"

"I had a date."

"Really… do tell."

"You remember the owner from Curvy Stitches, Zoey."

"No shit – her?"

"Why'd you say it like that?" Dawson appraised his fellow fireman.

"No reason. She's a hot redhead. I can see the allure. Hell, she's got some major curves."

"That she does." Dawson bit down on an apple.

"You know… if that health store had won the bid on that space, you might not have met her." Davis tapped the table.

"What are you talking about?"

"There were several offers on that corner spot. My dad is a councilman… he told me there was some serious bidding – but your girl won. I'm glad. We didn't need another health nut in town."

He shoveled some cereal into his mouth. Between bites, "I bet that chapped their asses – to lose to a curvy woman whose sole purpose is to sell to bigger women. Anyway… you're a lucky bastard if she's giving you the time of day. She's turned down a lot of guys in this town. A few of us thought she played for the other team."

Dawson tossed his apple core at his friend's head, "I can assure you she doesn't."

The bell, signaling a call for truck three and EMS, ended their conversation. Dawson hoped it would stay busy, making the workday go by faster so he could see Zoey again.

"Zoey Horton?" A massive bouquet hid the person calling out to her.

"That's me."

He set down the massive vase of roses, "Here ya go. These are for you. Have a great day." Zoey signed the delivery slip and waved as he exited her store.

> *These can't compete with your beauty... but then again, nothing can. I miss you. Looking forward to seeing you again.*
> *Dawson*

Zoey pressed her face to the massive arrangement and inhaled their floral scent. Every possible color of rose filled the ornate glass container. She set them on the counter where she could see them anywhere in the store.

"Those are beautiful." A customer setting her things on the counter pointed at the flowers, "You have one hell of a boyfriend."

"Oh... no, he's not my boyfriend. It's still new." Zoey blushed, thinking back to the passionate night they'd spent together.

"With that smile, I'd say it's headed that way."

Zoey shrugged. "This it for you?"

"For today," she laughed, "I have to say I am glad you opened and not another damn health store. Your shop is my favorite place to get clothes."

"Awe, thanks." Zoey bagged her items and handed her change back, "I'll be adding more to the collection soon."

"Great! I'll be back in a few weeks to check it out." The woman smiled, leaving Zoey alone in the store.

Pulling her phone out, she sent Dawson a quick text.

> Zoey: Got the flowers… they are beautiful.

> Dawson: Not nearly as beautiful as you.

Zoey's heart was beating wildly as she texted him back.

> Zoey: How's work?

> Dawson: Slammed…

Knowing it could get crazy at the firehouse, she didn't want to keep him tied up on the phone.

> Zoey: Well… won't keep you. Just want to say thank you. Be safe. See you tomorrow?

> Dawson: Definitely. xo

Zoey smiled at the kisses and hugs he sent; Dawson gave her butterflies. Something she never thought she'd have time for, but now, after finally giving him a shot – she couldn't help but feel giddy.

Turning to put her phone up, the sound of shattering glass made her jump. Spinning, she saw the front display window in shards on the floor.

"What the fuck?"

Running to the front of the store, she found a brick lying on the floor. Pressing her fingers to her temple, she let out a scream of frustration. Hurrying to the sidewalk, she looked around, finding the pavement empty.

"God damn it!" she bellowed into the sky.

Running back to the counter, she snatched her phone and called 9-1-1. She was starting to get pissed.

Why was her store being targeted?

CHAPTER 8

Dawson was glad to have a day off. He decided to surprise Zoey at work with coffee and donuts. He wasn't expecting to find a taped-up window when he got to her store.

Dread filled him, pulling open the door, "Zoey?"

Dawson stepped in, relief filling him when he spotted her at the counter.

"Hey, Dawson," Her smile didn't reach her eyes, she appeared deflated.

"What the hell happened?" Dawson set the coffee and donuts down on the counter and pulled her hand into his.

"Someone threw a brick through the window yesterday."

"You weren't hurt, were you?"

"Not physically… just my pride. I don't understand who is doing this." She squeezed her eyes shut.

Dawson reached across the counter and brushed a loose tendril of hair from her face, "Did the police come out?"

"Yes. I called them immediately. They took the brick but said chances of pulling any prints off are slim."

"You need me to fix the window?"

"No – someone is coming this afternoon to repair it. You brought coffee?"

"Thought I'd surprise you." Dawson released her hand and walked around the counter. He wrapped his arms around her, resting his chin on her head, "I'm sorry this is happening. It sure seems coincidental that your door was damaged, and now the window. Do you have any security cameras?"

"Just inside. I couldn't afford to put any outside."

"Well, that's better than none at all."

"Thanks, Dawson."

The door chimed as a customer came in, causing Zoey to jump back. Dawson laughed, "I'll let you get to work. Call me later – I'd like to see you soon."

"Same here. Maybe tomorrow? Tonight is my late night."

"Text me. We'll work it out." Dawson pressed a chaste kiss on her cheek and walked out. Zoey stared at the door, smiling at the man who'd very likely stolen her heart. That thought scared her. How was it possible to fall for someone after a few weeks of knowing them?

DAWSON SAT at the bar with his co-worker, Oren. Since Zoey was busy with work, he caved and agreed to meet him at the local brewery.

"Glad you decided to meet me. I do better with the ladies when I have a wingman." Oren laughed as he guzzled his beer.

"Glad to help… I guess." Dawson cocked an eyebrow at his friend. "Figured when you told the ladies you were a smoke jumper, they'd be falling at your boots."

Oren smiled as two blondes saddled up to the bar next to them. One of the girls tossed her hair and leaned into Dawson, "You two look lonely."

"Nope… well, maybe he is." Dawson thumbed towards Oren.

"Can I buy you a drink anyway?" She batted her eyes at Dawson.

"Sorry, ladies, my pal is off the market." Oren slid him another beer.

"Awe… really? I don't see her here." The flirty girl smiled.

"That's because she's working. Trust me, if she wasn't, she'd be with me." Dawson moved out of her reach.

"Working? It's nearly nine… who the hell works that late on a Tuesday?" She sneered.

"She does." Dawson turned to watch the T.V. in front of him.

"Yeah… his lady is the owner of Curvy Stitches." Oren smiled and threw his arm around the friendlier of the two ladies.

"*What*? That *fat* cow is your girlfriend."

"Watch what you say." Dawson crossed his arms over his chest and glared at her.

"Whatever, that bitch is the reason I couldn't open my store. She outbid me." She stomped her foot like a child, "Come on, Brandi, let's go."

Brandi, the blonde wrapped around Oren, smiled at him and apologized as she moved towards her friend. Dawson watched as the hateful woman walked out, practically dragging her friend behind her.

"Shit… maybe you aren't the one to use as a wingman." Oren laughed.

"Sorry, man. But that one was a real bitch."

CHAPTER 9

Dawson knocked on her door, excited to take her on an actual date. When she opened, she took his breath away. Standing there, she wore a tight navy blue dress that stopped above her knees. It hugged her curves in all the right places, leaving little to the imagination. Her legs were bare, except for the stunning pink high heels.

Dawson had to adjust himself, "Fuck… you're gorgeous."

"Thank you," Zoey giggled.

The sound sent a jolt right to his crotch. "Shall we?"

"Definitely. If we stand here too much longer, I'm going to push you back inside and take advantage of you."

Dawson grabbed her hand, leading her down the stairwell and outside. Hand in hand, they walked around the side of the building. Dawson spun her, pressing her back to the brick wall. Wedging his body against hers, he ravaged her mouth.

Zoey's hands fisted his hair, moaning into his mouth as he leaned into her.

Pulling back, "Sorry. I couldn't go another minute without kissing you."

Dawson helped her straighten her dress, "It's quite alright. I like that aggressive side of you." Zoey leaned forward and pressed her lips to his, "But I am starved. We can have dessert later." She turned, walking ahead of him towards downtown.

Dawson bit his lip as he followed behind her. He couldn't take his eyes off her. He'd be lucky to make it through dinner without wanting to take her on the table.

Zoey couldn't help the grin stretching across her face. She'd never felt this way with a man. Something about Dawson made her feel safe. He caught up with her, lacing his hand with hers, and walked toward a little Italian bistro down from her shop. Her store was downtown on main street, so she was close to everything.

The hostess seated them in a booth overlooking the beach. It was a picture-perfect date. Zoey looked out, gasping at the breathtaking view. The sky was laced with purple and pink ribbons as the sun descended. The water was smooth like glass, reflecting the colors filling the sky.

"Beautiful," Zoey whispered.

"Yes, you are."

She turned, a blush creeping up her neck, turning her cheeks a deep shade of red. "Thank you. But I was referring to the view."

"I know. But you're more beautiful than the view." Dawson strummed his thumb across her knuckles. He held her stare until the waiter broke their silent lust.

After they'd ordered, Zoey decided she wanted to learn more about him.

"So… I know you were in the military, but tell me about your family."

Dawson's jaw clenched, and Adam's apple bobbed as he swallowed. He took a deep breath, "It's just me. My parents died when I was eighteen. I think that's what made joining the military so easy."

"Oh, Dawson." Zoey slid her hand across the table, covering their already twined hands with it, "I'm sorry. We don't have to talk about it."

"No. It was a long time ago. I was eighteen when it happened. They'd gone out on our boat for Memorial Day. I didn't go because I had finals and needed to study. Truth be told, I just wanted to hang out with a girl. Funny thing is, I can't tell you her name now. Anyway…" He sipped water, "The police said it was quick. Another speed boat hit them, overturning theirs, killing them both on impact. My high school didn't make me walk or finish my finals. They just graduated me. I went and joined up two weeks later. What else was I supposed to do? I had no one. No family, no siblings. The military just seemed to fit."

Zoey could see the pain in his eyes, even though he did his best to hide the devastation he must have felt at such a young age.

"I know what it's like to lose a parent. But for you, to be young like that and lose both…" She sighed, "It's unfair and awful. Alright, let's change the subject to a happier one. What are you looking for in a relationship?"

"You." Dawson smiled, pulling her knuckles to his mouth. He pressed his lips to her skin.

"Seriously, Dawson. Are you looking for something semi-serious or casual, or are you looking for marriage? I'm just trying to get to know you."

"Well," Dawson smiled as the waiter placed their meals in front of them, "I don't do casual. I like to focus all my energy on one person, so serious, I guess. And marriage is always something I think about at my age; I mean, I'm not getting any younger. What about you? Do you want kids or a husband?"

"A husband, yes. Kids? Eventually maybe… I don't know; my business is just taking off, and I'm not sure kids would fit in right now. I mean – I'm not opposed to them eventually, but I am only twenty-five."

She watched as he took her words in, "Don't get me wrong, the right man could always change my mind." She cracked a smile, her eyes full of mischief when she spoke.

"And have you found the right guy?" His question was loaded, his gaze sending a spark to her core.

"Maybe."

Dawson paid the bill, "So, what would you like to do now?"

"I want dessert…" She cocked an eyebrow, knowing he knew what she meant, seeing as they paid the bill and were ready to walk out.

"You're place or mine?"

"Mine's closer." Zoey grabbed his hand, practically dragging him out of the restaurant.

They were both giggling as they approached her store.

"What the fuck," Dawson's growl startled Zoey. He pushed her behind his body in a protective stance.

"What… is something wrong."

Zoey peered around him. Her breath caught in her throat when she saw the window at the front of her shop. Someone had painted in big red letters *MINE*. It covered the entire length of the glass, the still-damp paint oozing down the pane and pooling on the sill.

CHAPTER 10

"WHAT IN THE EVER-LOVING FUCK?" ZOEY STEPPED AROUND Dawson, glaring at her windowpane.

"Why does this keep happening to me?"

She fisted her hair, pulling on her red locks. Dawson pressed his hand into her back, "Let's call the cops." He guided her to the curb and helped her sit down. Zoey could hear him on the phone with dispatch, her mind reeling over the new damage.

"Hey," Dawson sat beside her, "the police are on their way."

"I just don't get it, Dawson. Who is doing this?"

"I don't know. Could there be anyone mad at you?"

"Hell, I'm just a fat girl who keeps to herself. Maybe the girl who came in pissed off I stole her spot did this. I don't know." She pressed her head down into her hands and sighed.

"What, girl?"

"I don't know her name. She came in the day before I opened and told me I should close the shop. That no one wanted a fat girl shop."

"We'll tell the cops. Let them check into it. Maybe you should stay with me tonight…" Dawson looked over his shoulder at the paint-splattered sidewalk.

"No way. No one is running me out of my home. Plus, I thought you were going to stay here."

Dawson leaned into her side, "True."

The police arrived and took her statement and photographs of the message in red. They told her she was clear to wash it off and would contact her later in the week.

"Well, this isn't how I wanted to end our date."

"What do you mean?" Dawson helped her stand.

"Cleaning off my shop window. This sucks." Dawson followed her inside and helped her gather a bucket and supplies. Zoey filled the container with soapy water and grabbed a few extra towels.

Dawson took the bucket from her hands, "I don't know. Getting you all sudsy sounds sexy."

Zoey laughed, "Really? Because that's exactly what's going to happen. Maybe I should change." She glanced down at her dress.

"No… please don't. The thought of peeling that off wet is already getting me hard."

Dawson began scrubbing the glass, the red paint running down the street. Zoey moved alongside him, wiping and cleaning the hate speech spewed across the clear glass.

"I hate I'm ruining the sidewalk."

"Don't worry about it. I'll call the station in the morning and get them to hose it down."

"They'll do that?"

"For me? Of course." Dawson laughed.

Soon, the window was clean. On the other hand, the sidewalk looked like a small pig had been slaughtered.

"Well… I guess I can't do anything about the pavement. You ready to go upstairs?"

"Thought you'd never ask."

Dawson gathered all the cleaning supplies and carried them around back. Zoey let them in through the back door, pointing to the corner, "You can set that there. I'll take care of it tomorrow." She pulled the door closed and clicked the lock in place. She double-checked the shop door, ensuring it was locked tight, and headed up the stairs. "You coming?" She glanced at Dawson, still standing at the base of the steps.

Dawson snapped out of his trance and hurried up the stairs behind her. Zoey pushed through the door, Dawson hot on her tail.

He grabbed her, spinning her body against the door as it shut. He pressed into her, and his lips found hers. Zoey grabbed his shirt, tugging him towards her.

"I'm all wet. I should get out of this dress." She whispered into his lips.

"I should help you."

CHAPTER 11

Dawson slipped his fingers beneath the damp fabric, easing it over her head and tossing it to the floor. Zoey stood before him in a lacy thong and sheer bra. Dawson let out a growl before claiming her lips again.

Zoey tugged at his shirt, pleading with him to take it off. Dawson released her lips and tore them off. He lifted her body off the floor, her legs wrapping around his waist as he walked them to her bed. Dawson laid her down and kicked off his pants. His boxers clung to his muscular thighs, the outline of his arousal evident as he climbed over Zoey's body on the bed.

His mouth trailed a blaze of kisses up her flesh, licking and nipping at her skin. He settled between her legs, pressing his engorged member into her center as he attacked her mouth with his.

"Boxers… off." Zoey bucked her hips against the ridge of his cock. Dawson chuckled, leaning back as he eased the silky fabric down and tossed them to the floor. Sitting on his knees, he stroked his dick.

"What do you want, Zoey?" Dawson played with the crown of his cock, his free hand toying with Zoey's folds.

"You. Inside me. Now."

Dawson leaned forward, positioning himself at her entrance. He claimed her lips as he buried himself inside her channel. Zoey let out a hiss, her nails digging into his back as he seated himself fully inside her.

"God, you feel like heaven." Dawson started to move, easing himself out and ramming himself back in. Her cunt sucked his cock with each thrust. Zoey clawed at his flesh, moaning and writhing beneath him.

"Harder…" Zoey gasped out as Dawson pushed himself deeper. Dawson obliged by pressing harder, his hip bones slapping against her. His balls smacked against her ass as he thrust faster and more forcefully.

He could feel her core tightening around his member, her orgasm building as he lost himself inside her. Zoey cried out, her walls squeezing his dick. Dawson paused, relishing in the feel of her folds wrapped around him. Once her orgasm subsided, Dawson gripped her hips and flipped her over. Drawing her hips up, he shoved his cock inside her again.

Zoey moaned into the pillow, "FUCK…"

Dawson slapped her ass, drawing a hiss from her lips. He pounded her from behind, their grunts and moans filling the space of her loft apartment. Their bodies glistened with sweat as they fucked with abandon.

"I'm going to cum…" Zoey moaned, her pussy clenching and spasming around his dick. Dawson was near his release. He could feel his balls tighten as he drove inside her.

Zoey let out a piercing scream, her cunt milking his cock dry as he succumbed to her orgasm. His seed spurted inside her, filling her to the brim. Zoey collapsed to her belly, Dawson falling to the bed beside her.

"Wow." He mumbled, pulling her against his chest. "That was…"

"Amazing." Zoey giggled.

"Um… I should probably mention we forgot protection again." Dawson toyed with her loose curls.

"It's alright. I told you before I'm on the pill. So, as long as you're not doing this with someone else, I see no need to use them."

"With others?" Dawson leaned on his elbow, "Zoey, you're the only one I'm seeing." He kissed the tender flesh on her shoulder.

Zoey traced his stomach muscles with her finger, his skin rippled beneath her touch. Dawson grabbed her hand, halting her downward trail.

"Oh no, you don't." He rolled over, mounting her body. "I hope you're rested. Because I'm not done with you."

His tongue traced her collarbone, and Zoey's breath caught in her throat. She wiggled beneath him, her sex clenching in anticipation.

Dawson made his way between her legs, pushing her thighs open. He buried his fingers in her sweet center. He toyed with her, rubbing and flicking her G-spot.

Zoey cried out, her body spasming as she squirted her release. He pressed a kiss to her inner leg as he slipped his finger out. Zoey sat up, grabbing at his shoulder to pull him to her.

She pressed her mouth to his, their tongues tangling in a fury. Zoey could taste them both on his lips. Dawson crawled over her body, but Zoey had other plans. She shoved him back, straddling his waist.

"My turn."

Her eyes had a wicked gleam as she licked his chest. Swirling her tongue around his nipple, she nipped the pink flesh.

Dawson's hips bucked up, "Damn."

Zoey settled between his knees, her hands fisting his cock. She smiled as she stroked his member, eliciting a groan from Dawson. She pulled and tugged, leaning down to flick her wet tongue on his tip. She swirled her lips around his head, taking him deep into her throat.

Dawson couldn't stop the sounds coming from his chest. Her warm mouth felt like velvet on his cock. She bobbed her head, slurping as she tightened her hand at the base of his dick. She was like a madwoman bouncing her whole body as she sucked him hard.

"I'm going to cum." He tugged at her hair, warning her of his impending explosion. Zoey closed her lips harder around his engorged shaft. Dawson's balls contracted as his seed splashed into her throat. Zoey licked every drop, her lips making a pop sound as she pulled off his cock.

She climbed his body, settling into the crook of his arm, "You taste good."

Dawson laughed, "I think you broke me."

"Nah… you just need to rest." Zoey kissed his chest, "I'm sleepy too."

Dawson pulled her close, sleep claiming him as he snuggled into her body.

CHAPTER 12

THE LIGHT BURSTING THROUGH THE WINDOW WOKE ZOEY. She found herself wrapped in the warm blanket of Dawson's body. He was breathing softly, sleep still claiming him. Slowly, Zoey eased herself from his hold and padded her way to the bathroom.

She still held a post-sex glow when she looked at her reflection in the mirror. Peeking out at the man tangled in her sheets, she couldn't believe he was with her. She never thought someone like her could get a man like him. He was perfection. A man's man. Chiseled muscle, tattoos covering his chest, and a firefighter. She couldn't figure out what he saw in her for the life of her.

Turning on the shower, Zoey stepped beneath the warm spray. Her mind wandered back to their evening of lovemaking. He played her body like a well-tuned instrument. It was scary how well he seemed to know her needs.

The sound of the shower curtain sliding back startled Zoey. She smiled when arms wrapped around her waist.

"I woke up to an empty bed." Dawson pressed his lips to the sensitive spot behind her ear.

"I didn't want to wake you."

"You thought showering without me was a good idea?"

Dawson grabbed the shower poof and lathered it up with body wash. He ran the sudsy material down her backside, pausing to caress her ass.

"No…" Zoey breathed out, "I didn't think about it."

She spun to look into his eyes, "Dawson…" she pleaded.

Pressing his lips to hers, he backed her against the wall.

"I can't seem to get enough of you."

He ran his hand down her side and up her belly. He cupped her breast, pinching her nipple between his fingers.

Zoey closed her eyes and leaned her head against the cold tile. Her pussy clenched as his hand slid south. His fingers parted the tender flesh, burying themselves between her folds. Gripping her shoulder, he pumped his fingers in and out. His kiss was feral as he drew her orgasm to the surface.

"FUCK… you're so wet." He kissed the hollow of her neck.

"I want you inside me, Dawson."

Dawson hoisted her up, Zoey's legs wrapped around him instinctively. His cock sought her cunt, teasing the outside of her lips. With one thrust, her pussy swallowed his cock. Their sex was fast and hard. They chased their pleasure as the water cascaded down their bodies. The slapping of skin and splashing of water filled the tiny space. Zoey screamed out. Dawson grunted as his cum filled her womb. Zoey's muscles clenched around his morning erection as they reached their blissful state together.

"Damn, woman." Dawson set her on her feet, "I think I'm addicted to you."

"And that's a problem?"

"Nope… not at all."

Zoey giggled as they finally washed each other. Dawson stepped out, wrapping a towel around his waist.

Zoey dried off and sauntered to her bed, "I need to get dressed and downstairs. I'm supposed to open in an hour."

"How about I get dressed and go grab us some breakfast? I can bring it to the store."

"Sure… that would be amazing."

Dawson threw on his clothes from last night and pulled Zoey in for a hug. "Be back in a few."

"Great. Meet you downstairs."

Zoey hurried to dress, pulling her hair into a sleek ponytail. Grabbing her keys, she ran down the back stairs. She locked the back door. Dawson had gone out and slipped into the store through the rear entrance.

Walking to the front, she flicked on the lights and grabbed the mail gathered at the mail slot. Unlocking the door, a letter in the stack stood out. There was no return address; it only had her name on the front.

She set the rest of the mail down and pulled the envelope out. Ripping it open, she slid out the folded paper inside. She couldn't believe the words written. They were vile and hateful. Zoey clenched the torn envelope in her hand, the words cutting her like a knife.

CHAPTER 13

"Zoey?" Dawson's voice snapped her from the trance she was under. "What the hell?" He grabbed the letter from her hand.

```
I'll have what's mine eventually.
Enjoy the fun now… it won't last.
```

"Who sent this, Zoey?"

"I… I don't know." She pressed her hands to her face, "Why is this happening?"

"Have there been others? Zoey, I'm calling the police. They need to know you got this. I mean," Dawson paced, "This, plus the damage to your shop, is starting to freak me out."

"I know. God, this is infuriating."

"Zoey!" The sound of the door and her mother's sing-song voice made Zoey wince.

"Mom," Zoey gave Dawson an apologetic grin, "What are you doing here?"

"Well, I haven't heard from you in a few days, so I thought I'd stop by to check on you. But I can see what has you so busy…" She turned to Dawson, "Hello, I'm Katrina Horton, Zoey's mom. And you are?"

Dawson held his hand out, "Dawson Ford, ma'am. A pleasure to meet you. I can see where Zoey gets her looks."

"My, my. A charmer. And what do you do, Dawson?"

"I'm a firefighter. Station three."

"Oh… nice. Alright, well… I can see you're busy. How about dinner tonight? You can bring your friend, Zoey." Katrina smiled at her daughter.

"Sure. I'll call you later, Mom." She pressed a kiss to her mom's cheek.

Dawson watched her mother leave the store before turning to Zoey, "OK. Now, can we call the police?"

"Yeah… fine." Zoey busied herself getting things in order with the store. She was pissed this was happing to her. For the life of her, she couldn't understand why someone had targeted her or the store.

Zoey wanted to scream. Just when her life was coming together, this shit was interfering with her peace.

"Miss Horton?" A man dressed in a blue polo, marked with police, stood at her counter.

"Yes. That's me."

"I'm from the department. Someone called and said you'd received a threat of some sort?"

"Yes." Zoey handed him the note, "I found this mixed in with my mail this morning."

"Interesting. And you've had some recent vandalism to the shop as well?"

"That's correct. It started with the door being busted. Then the brick through the window and then the window was painted with MINE in red paint. This isn't the first letter I've gotten either."

"What?" Dawson stood behind her, "What do you mean this isn't the first letter? Why didn't you tell me about the others?"

"There was just one other. I'll go grab it." Zoey hurried to her office; searching through the drawer, she found the letter she'd crumbled and shoved to the back.

"Here," she handed the letter to the Detective.

He read the note, comparing it to the newest one.

"The notes and damage don't come right out and threaten you directly, but it's implied. Is there someone angry with you? And ex-boyfriend, perhaps?"

Zoey snorted, "No… I don't date."

Dawson cleared his throat, cocking an eyebrow at her.

"Well, not until you. Are you mad at me?"

She gave him a cheeky grin.

"Not funny," Dawson growled. "What about that woman who gave you shit the first day you were open?"

"Woman?" The detective asked.

"Yeah, this woman came into the shop the day before I opened. She told me no one wanted me here, and I should just close the store. But I haven't heard from her since."

"Do you know her name?"

"No."

"Wait," Dawson tapped the counter, "I ran into her at the bar. I didn't get her name, but she was with another girl she called Brandi. She complained that you're the reason she couldn't open her store because you'd won the bid to this place."

"Alright. I'll do some digging and see if I can find her. Until then, be vigilant and let me know if anything else happens."

He handed Zoey his card and shook Dawson's hand before leaving.

"Here," Dawson slid the box of donuts towards Zoey, "Let's eat these and talk about how to handle this problem."

"Seriously, Dawson? Problem? There is nothing to talk about. The police will figure this out."

"Zoey, you need to take this seriously."

"I am. I'm just not going to let it make me run scared. Now… give me that jelly-filled donut." She snatched the powdered donut from his hand and shoved it into her mouth.

They sat together, discussing the shop, her mother, and their next date. Dawson was on edge about the things happening, but Zoey had made it clear she didn't want to dwell on the matter.

Zoey invited him to her mother's for dinner, but he had to be on shift early the following day. They agreed to go on a date Tuesday after she closed the shop.

Dawson kissed her goodbye, promising to stop in if he could while on duty. Zoey watched him as he walked away. She couldn't help but worry something was wrong. Someone as perfect as him shouldn't be with someone like her.

CHAPTER 14

ZOEY SAT ACROSS FROM HER MOTHER AT THE DINNER TABLE. Her suspicious glare made Zoey uncomfortable.

"Why are you staring at me like that, Mom?"

"Just wondering what is going on with you and that hunky fireman."

"We're dating. It's new." Zoey popped a tomato in her mouth, the juice dripping onto her chin when she bit down. Grabbing her napkin, she wiped the remnants from her skin.

"Huh." Her mom smiled, "He seems nice."

"He is. But like I said. It's new. He'll get bored of me eventually. I'm sure."

"What? Why would you say that, Zoey?"

"Mom. Seriously, look at me and look at him. We don't exactly match. Someone he is more suited with will eventually catch his eye."

"Zoey… I don't know why you're so hard on yourself. You are a beautiful woman. If he's the right man for you, there won't be any other women for him. And based on how he looked at you, I'd like to believe he's the one. So tell me, how's business? Anything new happening?"

"I had some more vandalism. The police department is investigating."

"What – why didn't you call me?"

"Mom, I'm an adult. I think I can handle a little vandalism on my own."

"You may be an adult, but you're still my daughter. And I have a right to worry. When you have your own child, you'll understand."

"Whatever… look. I need to head home. It's getting late, and I have a shop to run in the morning."

"Promise you'll call me if something else happens?"

"Yes, mother."

Zoey hugged her mom goodbye and climbed into her car. Even though she nagged her, Zoey loved her mother with all her heart. It was the two of them against the world for so long. If it hadn't been for her pushing Zoey to do what she wanted in her life, she would have never had the courage to become a business owner.

Zoey locked her door, checking to ensure everything was secure at the shop before retiring to bed. She'd texted Dawson a few times during dinner with her mom. She missed having him around. She was falling for him, and it scared her.

Her ringing phone startled her.

"Hey, Dawson."

"How was dinner with your mom?"

"Good. She wants you to join us next time."

"Maybe we could meet her for dinner one night this week."

"She'd like that," she smiled at Dawson.

Zoey was happy he was willing to spend time with her mom. Her last boyfriend tried to put a wedge between her and her mom – that had been the final straw in their relationship.

"As much as I'd like to spend the night on the phone with you, I have to be up early. Can I call you in the morning?"

"Of course. Get some rest. I'll talk to you tomorrow, Dawson."

"Sleep tight, Zoey."

"I will." She disconnected the call and slipped into bed.

Dawson strolled into the station right on time. He'd nearly overslept, his mind wouldn't turn off – his thoughts on Zoey.

"Hey, Ford... how was your weekend?" Uri hollered from the couch.

"Good, yours?"

"Pretty damn awesome, if I might say so. I met some hot chick at the bar Saturday night. You should have been there."

"No, thanks. I had a date."

"A date – with that curvy girl?"

Dawson growled at his partner, "Watch it, Uri."

"I don't mean it in a bad way, geez."

Dawson's phone vibrated in his pants; pulling it from his pocket, he smiled when he saw Zoey's face across the screen.

"Hey." He flicked Uri off as he headed towards the front of the station.

"Hey, you." Zoey giggled into the phone.

"Everything good at the shop?"

"Yep. Already had a few customers this morning. And no vandalism. That's a good start to the day. How about you? Any calls yet?"

"Nah. I just got here. The other shift just left. They said they had a slow night, which means it'll be crazy for us. That's usually how it works."

"Well, if you get a chance to stop by, I'll be here."

The tone sounded in the background, signaling a call.

"Well… It looks like it's time for me to go to work. Call you later?"

"Of course. And Dawson," Zoey inhaled, "be careful."

"Always."

Dawson pocketed his phone and jogged to the truck. They were being dispatched to a car accident, so time was of the essence.

"You got it bad, brother." Oren slapped him on the back.

"Yeah. I think I do." Dawson grinned, climbing into the rig next to his team members. He was sure he was in love with Zoey, but he knew she was skittish and needed to take it slowly with her. When the time was right, he'd tell her how he felt.

CHAPTER 15

THE DAY BLEW BY, KEEPING ZOEY BUSY FOR THE LATTER half. As the sky turned dark, she locked up the storefront and headed upstairs. She was exhausted, and between the few texts from Dawson, she knew he had been slammed at work.

She tossed a frozen dinner in the microwave and headed into the bathroom. She hopped in the shower and quickly rinsed the day off. Slipping on some leggings and a T-shirt, she headed back into the kitchen just in time for the microwave to ding.

She sat down, flicked on the TV, and settled in to watch Grey's Anatomy. Zoey had missed the last several episodes, so she was eager to see what had been happening.

After sending a quick text to Dawson, she plugged her phone up and set it on the counter. Settling in on the couch, she let herself doze off to the noise of the TV in the background.

ZOEY WOKE WITH A START. Something seemed off in the apartment. Wiping the sleep from her eyes, she stood and went to the sink. She couldn't shake the feeling that something was wrong. Deciding to check on the store, she pulled on the door, intending to go downstairs. She was shocked to find it wouldn't budge.

"What the fuck?"

She pulled harder, confused as to what kept the door shut. She peered out the window, noticing a strange glow in the night sky. Squinting harder, she gasped when she realized the light was actually a fire in her shop.

She scrambled back to the door, tugging on it with all her might. No matter how hard she pulled it, it would not budge.

Zoey caught the faint whiff of smoke seeping in beneath the door jam. She dropped to her knees, peering under the tiny crack only to see the same orange glow outside.

She scooted backward, panic setting in. Her shop was on fire, and she was trapped in her apartment. She stood, rushing to the counter where she'd set her phone.

"9-1-1, what is your emergency?"

"Yes… my name is Zoey Horton. I live at 2216 Court Street, in the apartment above Curvy Stitches. My store is on fire, and I am trapped in the apartment. Please… send someone."

"Ma'am, is there any way you can get out?"

"No, the windows do not open, and the door is jammed. Please… Oh god… the smoke."

"Ok. I need you to listen to me. Go into the bathroom and wet some towels. Place them in front of the door. Can you do that?"

"Yes…hold on." Zoey set the phone down and rushed to do what the dispatcher said. "Ok… I did that… but it is getting hot in here. Is the fire department on the way?"

"Ma'am, they've been dispatched. Stay on the phone with me. Go back to the bathroom and cover yourself in a wet towel."

Zoey ran into the bathroom, grabbed a towel, and turned on the shower. She set the phone down. The smoke had doubled in quantity. Zoey could smell the unmistakable scent of burning wood. Peering into the living room, she saw flames had breached the closed door and converged up the wall.

Closing her eyes, she prayed for someone to save her. Her lungs began to burn, and her head began to swirl. Zoey felt her eyes droop as she succumbed to the smoke filling her breath.

CHAPTER 16

When the bell rang, Dawson had just kicked his feet up on the coffee table.

"Station three, all units. Signal 33 – structure fire. Respond to 2216 Court Street – Curvy Stitches. Be advised, the caller on the scene is trapped."

Dawson nearly stumbled over himself.

"*What the fuck*? Uri!" Dawson bellowed his partner's name as he ran towards the rig, "Did I hear that right? Curvy Stitches is on fire?"

"Yeah… isn't that your girl's place?"

"Yes… she lives above the shop." He shot his friend a panicked expression.

"Hey," Oren rested his hand on Dawson's arm, "We'll get her."

Dawson geared up and held on as his Lieutenant drove balls to the wall to the call. Dawson could hardly contain himself when they arrived. He bolted from the truck, stopping on the curb. He couldn't believe what he was seeing. The entire shop was engulfed in orange flames. Smoke billowed high into the night sky as embers of wood floated into the darkness.

"Alright. We need to find a way in." Lt. Hill barked out orders, "Oren, Kristof – you two get a line started on this inferno. Dawson, you're with me. You know of another way to the apartment?"

"Around back."

Dawson took off in a sprint, the yell of the LT warning him to wait in the distance. He slipped his mask in place, securing the helmet on his head before he kicked the door open with his boot. The wood crumbled under his fury.

Dawson didn't pause to wait for Hill. Zoey was inside, so he wasn't going to waste time waiting for orders. He was enraged at what he found when he reached the top of the steps. A bar had been wedged in the door jam, preventing it from being opened from either direction. The flames licked at his back, the heat pressing against his turnout gear. Using the heel of his boot, he kicked the bar loose. With all his might, he rammed the door open with his shoulder.

The fire had already spread to the interior of her apartment. The entire front of the loft was fully engulfed. Dawson scanned the room, feeling his anxiety spike when he didn't see Zoey anywhere.

"Zoey!" He called out, his breaths coming out as a grunt as he fought the smoke. He kicked the couch out of the way, shoving it with his knee.

"Dispatch," Dawson barked into his radio, "what was the caller's last known location?"

"I instructed her to go into the bathroom."

Dawson rushed towards the only room in the loft apartment. He pushed the door open. The wind nearly knocked out of him when he spotted Zoey passed out in the bathtub. The spray of the shower poured down on her still body. Although she was wet, her face was covered in soot, and she appeared to be barely breathing.

"ZOEY!"

"DAWSON!" He heard Lt. Hill hollering for him inside the apartment, "We gotta go… this place is coming down."

Dawson tugged Zoey into his arms and slipped his mask and helmet off. He pressed the respirator to her face, "Come on, baby. Breathe."

Tucking her into his chest, he wrapped his jacket around them, not caring that he was getting wet. Tugging his helmet and respirator back on, he ran toward the stairs, her body firmly secure against his.

Lt. Hill met him at the entrance, "Let's go." He went to pull her from his arms, but Dawson held fast.

"I got her."

As they hurried down the steps, the roof began to crumble. Wood splintered and cracked as Dawson stepped into the night air. He carried her limp body away from the burning embers and set her in the grass.

"Please, Zoey. MEDIC…"

Dawson screamed into the night air. He pressed his ear to her chest, listening for any sign of life.

"Please…" he pressed her chest, breathing air into her lungs.

"Hey… Let me do this, Dawson."

Corey Davis pushed Dawson to the side. Dawson fell to his butt, watching as the EMT's worked on the woman who'd stolen his heart.

"Please…" Dawson watched helplessly as they worked on her body. Tears streaked down his cheeks, leaving a trail in the caked-on black soot.

"We got a pulse," Corey motioned to the others, motioning for them to load her on the stretcher. "Let's go."

Helen, his partner, grabbed Dawson's arm, "You can ride with us. They've got this fire under control."

Dawson nodded, following them as they rushed her towards the ambulance. Dawson climbed into the back of the rig, watching as Helen continued to work on her.

"Will she be ok?"

"She's got a strong pulse…"

"That's not an answer, Helen."

"Look, Dawson. You know as well as I do. We won't know until they check her out. But she's young. You got to her in time."

Dawson pulled her hand into his, "What the fuck happened."

"I don't know, Dawson. But I overheard Captain saying it looked like the fire had been set intentionally."

"Someone tried to kill her?"

"Looks that way."

"Fuck."

Dawson held her hand in his the whole way to the hospital. He watched as the doctor wheeled her into the back, leaving him to stare at the doors as they closed in his face.

He walked back to the waiting room and slumped into a chair. Slipping his phone from his pocket, he called dispatch. Her mother was listed as an emergency business contact. Dawson wanted to call her himself.

Dawson drew in a deep breath, "Ms. Horton? It's Dawson. There's been an accident. You need to meet me at the hospital."

After briefly explaining what happened, he disconnected the call. He closed his eyes and prayed for the first time in a long time.

He needed Zoey to wake up.

He needed to tell her how he felt.

CHAPTER 17

Zoey felt like she was floating. She couldn't remember what she was doing. She just knew it was hot. Strong arms wrapped around her, lifting her. Her body was on fire. Her lungs burned.

Where was she?

Why was it so hot?

She thought she heard someone calling her name, but was she dreaming?

Her head hurt... she was so tired.

Closing her eyes, she gave in to the darkness.

DAWSON SAT by Zoey's bed, her mother opposite him. Katrina Horton showed up to the emergency room shortly after Dawson called her. He hadn't even changed clothes. He was still dressed in his turn-out gear, his jacket slung over the chair he sat in. His face was covered in soot, his shirt drenched in sweat.

"Why isn't she waking up?" Dawson asked the nurse, taking her vitals.

"It's not uncommon for fire victims to remain unconscious while their body heals. Give her time. Her vitals are good, and her heart is strong."

"Dawson," Captain Pountz stepped into her room, "How is she?"

"Stable, but still unconscious."

"Ma'am," he glanced at Zoey's mom, "I think you should know the fire was set intentionally. Investigators are still on scene trying to gather evidence."

"Who would do this to her?"

"This is so fucked up." Dawson ran his fingers through his hair.

"Look, you should go home and get cleaned up. You're covered in soot and ash."

"I don't want to leave her, Cap."

"Dawson," Katrina stood, "Go. Leave me your number. I'll call you if something changes with her condition."

Dawson stood, reluctant to leave. He leaned over and pressed a kiss to her forehead, "Fine. I won't be gone long. Call me if she wakes up."

"Thank you." Katrina hugged him, "She's lucky you got there in time. I don't know what I would do if she had been…" Katrina muffled a sob as Dawson tugged her into a hug.

"She's going to be alright."

"Thank you."

"I'll see you in a bit. You have my number."

Dawson glanced one last time at Zoey's still form in the bed. She looked so peaceful, but he wouldn't relax until she woke up and he could look into her beautiful eyes again.

CHAPTER 18

It felt like an elephant was perched on her forehead, tap dancing. Every breath she took sent a piercing pain through her chest. There was a fog she couldn't seem to shake from her brain.

"Ughhhh…" She let out a soft groan, her voice raspy and burning as she tried to speak.

"Zoey…" Someone said her name. "Someone go get the doctor."

That voice. She knew that voice. Why couldn't she open her eyes?

"Zoey," rough fingers danced along her face, brushing her hair from her cheek. "Darlin, can you open your eyes?"

"Dawson," she squeaked out, her throat burning. Her eyelids were heavy as she tried to pry them open. Blinking, the light burned as her vision adjusted. Glancing around the room, she saw her mother at her feet. Dawson was at her side, holding her hand in his.

"Where…., Where am I?" Zoey squeezed her eyes shut when the memory of flames assaulted her, taking her breath away. "Oh. My. God. My store?"

"It's going to be alright, Zoey." Her mom patted her leg, "All that matters is you're safe and alive." Katrina sucked in a sob, "I almost lost you."

"Is it gone?"

Dawson sat beside her, his palm cupping her cheek, "You can rebuild. All that matters is you're awake now. God, Zoey. I thought I'd lost you in that fire."

"You saved me." It wasn't a question. Zoey already knew it was him… the angel that pulled her from the inferno.

"If I'd been a moment later…" his voice drifted off, his eyes dipping to the bed.

"But you weren't." Zoey tightened her fingers in his. "Do they know what happened?"

"Arson." Her mother's words were bitter on her tongue.

"Arson?"

"Well… it looks like you've decided to join us." The doctor cut off her question, pushing into the room. "Let's check you over."

For the next fifteen minutes, he reviewed her vitals and gave them instructions on aftercare. Since there were no outward injuries, she would be released – pending the blood work didn't show anything nefarious.

"You'll stay with me." Her mother spoke, standing to start gathering her things.

"Mom…" Zoey pinched her nose.

"What? Your apartment is gone, Zoey. Your things are gone. Where else would you go?"

"With me. She can stay with me." Dawson glanced between the two women, "Zoey, let me take care of you."

"Dawson… that's sweet, but mom's right. I'll be fine at her house."

Dawson stood, "Well, the offer still stands. Let me at least drive you home."

"That works out well. " Katrina pulled off her house key and handed it to him, "take her to my house so I can grab some essentials for her. I will meet you in a few hours. I'll bring dinner, so plan on staying, Dawson."

Katrina kissed Zoey and left them alone to wait on the discharge papers.

"Dawson," Zoey cocked her head, a slight headache still pounding against her temple, "You said they suspect arson caused the fire?"

"Yes. It's still early in the investigation, but everything points to it being intentionally set."

"Why?" Zoey couldn't stop the tears from falling, "Who would do this to me?"

Dawson sat beside her, pulling her into his arms. He held her close while she let the emotions pour out of her.

"I don't know, Zoey. But the police are investigating this. They'll figure it out."

"My whole life's gone up in flames. It was all I had, Dawson."

"No, it wasn't, Zoey. You have your mom. Hell," he pulled back to look into her eyes, "You have me." His lips captured hers in a heartfelt kiss.

"You should cut your losses, Dawson." She pulled away from him, looking out the window of her hospital room.

"What? Why would you say that?"

"Look at me. I'm just some fat girl with nothing now. You don't deserve the headache I bring."

"Shut up."

His words bit more than he meant, but he needed her to hear him.

"Zoey… I don't care about what's happening. But I do care about you. So help me God, if I hear you say you're fat one more time…"

Zoey scooted out of bed, standing slowly, "You'll what?"

Dawson was on her in a millisecond, "I'll show you how beautiful you are until you believe it because you're beautiful, Zoey. Damn, you're insufferable." He pulled her to him, his arms wrapping around her body. "Let's get you changed so we can go home."

"Changed into what? All my clothes were burned, remember?"

"I brought you some of my sweats—here…" he reached beneath the bed and pulled out a bag.

"Thanks."

Zoey took the bag and hurried into the bathroom. Staring at her reflection, she saw a broken, angry woman looking back.

CHAPTER 19

ZOEY PEERED OUT THE WINDOW OF HER MOTHER'S KITCHEN. This had been her home for most of her childhood. It held memories that were both good and bad. Now… sitting here because someone had burned her entire life down meant she had nothing but time to think about her life.

"Zoey?" Her mom pulled a chair up beside her. "Honey, you need to get out. You've holed yourself up inside since the accident. It's not healthy. And don't think I haven't noticed you're avoiding that handsome man of yours."

"Mom… I need some time."

"Ok—but can't you take time with him? That man saved your life."

"It was his job, mother."

"Don't give me that. Sure… he's a fireman, but that man ran into that building, ignoring his captain's orders to get to you. He didn't care that he could potentially lose his life, too. And not only that…" she stood and went to the sink, "He stayed by your bedside the entire time you were unconscious. Now try and tell me you were just a job, Zoey."

Zoey laid her head down on the table. Her mother was right. She'd been hiding from Dawson since he brought her home. They'd exchanged text messages, but she'd asked him for some time, and he'd complied. Although he texted her daily that he missed her.

"I'll text him. You're right, Mom; I've been avoiding him."

"Why?"

"He doesn't deserve to be caught up in this mess."

"I don't think that's your decision to make. That man cares about you. I venture to say he even loves you."

"Loves me? Mom, we've only been dating a few weeks."

But even as she said the words, Zoey's heart did a pitter-patter. Before the fire, she'd come to terms with the fact that she was falling for him, so it wasn't so farfetched that he could be falling for her, too. Then her self-doubt trickled in, telling her she wasn't good enough for a man like him. Zoey had a hard time believing Dawson could love her.

"Stop." Her mother threw a dishtowel at her, "Call him."

Zoey pushed back, stood, and grabbed her phone. Her mom had picked up a new one for her while she'd been in the hospital. Fortunately, she had backed up all her settings to the cloud, so nothing had been lost.

Stepping outside, Zoey sat down on the stairs of the front porch. Her mother's house backed up to the water, giving her a beautiful ocean view.

Zoey smiled at Dawson's contact picture. Pressing the phone to her ear, she waited.

"Zoey." His voice filled the line, "You ok?"

"I'm good. Are you busy?"

"Not for you."

"I'd like to see you, Dawson. I owe you an apology for how I've been acting."

"You owe me nothing, woman. I'll be there in ten minutes."

The line went dead, leaving Zoey to stare blankly at the screen. Closing her eyes, she wished things were back to normal. Everything had been going well until the fire. She still couldn't understand why someone would target her like they had.

CHAPTER 20

Dawson nearly broke every law driving to see Zoey. Over the last two weeks, he'd kept his distance. Dawson understood she needed time to deal with everything, but he didn't like being away from her. He needed her to know how he felt but had yet to tell her. Dawson was afraid his admission would frighten her. Hell, admitting it to himself was scary enough.

His heart began to beat wildly when he pulled into the driveway. Zoey sat on the top step, her fiery red hair blowing in the slight breeze from the ocean.

She stood to greet him as he stepped out of his truck. "Dawson."

"Zoey," he tugged her into his arms, wrapping her in a tight hold. "I've missed you."

"I've missed you, too."

She snuggled against him, inhaling his fresh scent. It was a mixture of wood and laundry detergent.

"Want to take a walk with me?"

Dawson laced their fingers together, tugging her along the sidewalk down to the beach. Zoey paused, slipped her shoes off, and tossed them to the back deck. Dawson followed suit and rolled his pant legs up.

"How have you been?"

"Lost." Zoey glanced at the horizon.

"What do you mean, lost?"

"Everything that's happened has my whole life flipped upside down. I don't even know where to begin."

"How about at the beginning? I know this is hard, but Zoey— you can start over. I'll help you."

"Why would you do that, Dawson?"

He spun her to face him, "Zoey, meeting you has been the best thing to happen to me in a long time. And this stupid fire isn't going to derail this relationship."

"Relationship? Is that what we have?"

She held her breath, fear holding her hostage as she waited for his response.

"Yes… relationship. Look, Zoey. I planned on telling you on our date, but the fire fucked that up. I'm falling in love with you… and I don't want to miss seeing what could become of us together."

Zoey blinked, "You're falling in love with me?"

"No…I mean, yes—actually," Dawson kissed her lips, "I am in love with you, Zoey. And I realize it may be too soon for you, but I needed you to know how I felt."

Zoey's eyes misted with tears. Lost for words, all she could do was stare at him. Dawson had saved her life not just from the fire but from a life of never being loved.

"I…," she sucked in a breath, "I'm in love with you, too." Her words carried along with the breeze as it whipped through her hair.

"What?" Dawson cupped her cheeks, "You love me too?"

She nodded, "Yes…now what?"

"Come home with me. Let me make you dinner. Spend the night with me, please."

"I've never seen your place."

"Because we never seemed to make it out of yours." He laughed.

"Let me go gather some things and let my mother know. She'll worry if I leave and not tell her."

"I'd like to say hello anyway."

Zoey started toward the house, but Dawson halted her movement. He captured her lips in a searing kiss that sent fire straight to her core. Her womb clenched with need, her center burning for his touch.

"Now, we can go."

Dawson and Zoey hurried up the pathway together. After speaking with her mother and giving her time to gather some clothes, Zoey watched the scenery as they drove towards Dawson's.

"I live on the other side of town. I bought a two-bedroom bungalow on the water when I moved here. It's similar to your mom's… just not as big."

"How did we never come here before?" Zoey's eyes were wide with wonder as she took in the tiny home he called his. It was charming and had the most beautiful view of the water.

"It was on the to-do list." He smiled, cutting off the engine. "Let me give you a tour."

"Dawson… as much as I'd like a tour of the place," She bit her bottom lip, "The only room I care about right now is your bedroom."

CHAPTER 21

They'd barely made it into the house before stripping off their clothes. Dawson hoisted Zoey against him as he carried her through the house. She'd pulled her dress off between the front door and his bedroom.

Dawson laid them down on the bed, his body engulfing hers as he planted a trail of kisses down her chin. He licked and nibbled at her tender flesh, causing her to buck against him.

"I need you naked." He whispered into her ear as he tugged at her panties. Zoey lifted her hips, allowing him to pull the lacy fabric down her thighs. She snagged his shirt, ripping it over his head as he stood to remove his pants.

Zoey bit her lip as she took in his sculpted body. "God, you're gorgeous." She giggled as she ran her fingernails along the plains of his stomach.

Dawson laced their fingers together as he pushed her arms above her head. He kissed her hard, pressing his erection into her hot center. Zoey wrapped her legs around his back, begging him to enter her.

"Please!"

Dawson's cock eased into her folds, his breath quickening as her muscles tightened around his shaft. "Fuck…" He hissed.

Their movements became frantic. Their bodies met in a frenzy like the ocean crashing into the shore. Dawson gripped her hip, his fingers digging into her skin as he pressed his cock deeper. Zoey begged and pleaded, urging him to give it to her harder.

"I'm going to cum…" she tilted her head back, giving him access to her neck. Dawson bit down, suckling her throat as she tumbled over the edge. He slowed his movements, pausing to enjoy the sensation of her cunt pulsing around his shaft.

Rolling over, Dawson shifted Zoey above him. He speared his cock into her again, eliciting a moan from her. Her juices coated his cock, dripping down his painfully hard dick.

"Fuck me, Zoey…" she bucked and bounced, "That's it, baby. Ride my cock. I want to feel you cum on me again. Suck my shaft inside that tight little pussy of yours."

Zoey rode him with abandon. Rocking into his pelvis, chasing her orgasm. She tilted her head back, crying out his name as her walls spasmed around him, squeezing out his essence.

"Fuck… I'm going to fill you up, baby."

Dawson spurted his load into her womb, his seed relentlessly searching for a place to take root. His cock jerked inside her as her pussy clamped down on what it wanted. She collapsed onto his chest, her breath coming out in bursts of strangled air.

"Fuck… I needed that."

"Me too, baby."

Dawson pulled her to his side, snuggling against her. "I love you, Zoey."

"I love you too."

"Let's rest a bit, then I can fix you some food, ok?"

"Sounds good to me." Zoey started to drift off, her heart content to be wrapped in his arms again. Soon, his slow breathing matched hers as they lay there, wrapped in a cocoon of love.

A LOUD CRASH woke Zoey from her post-sex haze.

"Dawson," She poked him in the side, rousing him from his slumber, "Something just crashed outside."

"What?"

He shook the sleep from his eyes just as another loud bang vibrated through the house. "Stay here."

He jumped up, grabbed his discarded pants, and pulled them on. He ran from the bedroom, Zoey frantically tugging her dress on to follow behind him.

Dawson skidded to a halt as he yanked open the front door. He couldn't believe what he was seeing. His truck windshield had been shattered; shards of glass covered the ground.

Dawson grabbed his shoes that sat by the door, "Wait here."

"No. I'm coming with you."

Zoey slipped her sandals on and stepped onto the porch with Dawson.

"Call 9-1-1, Zoey."

Zoey dialed the number, asking for dispatch to send a unit. Dawson eased off the steps, edging towards his truck. He scanned the area, looking for who had done the damage.

As he stepped closer to the driver's side, he spotted a note taped to the window.

I will get what is mine.

"What the hell," Zoey attempted to snatch the letter from the glass, but Dawson grabbed her hand.

"Don't touch it, Zoey."

He pulled her into his side, "I don't see anyone out here, but stay close."

"I don't understand."

As she buried her head in his side, a patrol car pulled up. For the next several minutes, Zoey and Dawson recounted what they knew. The officer took the letter as evidence, telling them that the detective would likely stop by later to talk with them some more. After he took photos of the damage,

Dawson covered the opening with a tarp he'd retrieved from his garage.

"Let's go inside. I'm hungry."

Dawson guided her up the steps. The sound of the door slamming made Zoey jump. Dawson was pissed. Zoey worried he would see the relationship as too much trouble – making him leave her for good.

CHAPTER 22

"I'll call my mother." Zoey walked around Dawson, searching for her discarded purse.

"Why are you calling her?"

"To come to get me. You shouldn't have to deal with this, Dawson. Now your property has been damaged... it's my fault."

"Hold up, Zoey." He grabbed her arm, "I'm mad. Yes... but not at you. I'm pissed that the police are nowhere closer to figuring out who is doing this and why. I am pissed that someone is tormenting you and nearly killed you in a fire. I. Am. Not. Angry. With. You." He pulled her in for a kiss.

A knock at the door startled her, causing Zoey to jump in his arms.

"Stay here." Dawson walked to the door, relieved to see it was the detective.

"Detective," He motioned for him to step inside.

"Miss Horton, Mr. Ford."

"Detective, do you have any more information for me?" Zoey smiled timidly at the man.

"Yes. I have a few questions first. Can we sit?" He motioned to the table.

"Sure…" Zoey walked to the table and sat down. Dawson stood behind her, his hands resting on her shoulders.

"Zoey, what can you tell me about Marco Stephens?"

"Marco?" Zoey pressed her hand to her head, "He's an ex-boyfriend."

"When was the last time you talked to him?"

"Two years ago, why?"

"Were you aware of his history?"

"I…," she glanced at Dawson, confused at why she was being asked about an ex-boyfriend.

"Detective, what does this have to do with anything?" Dawson stroked her neck, trying to relieve the tension he could see.

"Marco Stephens has an extensive history. Stalking, aggravated assault, arson, just to name a few. We believe he's been following you for some time now."

"What?" Zoey shook her head.

"Zoey… did he ever give you any indication he was dangerous?"

"God… this is so confusing. Marco and I dated for about two years. I broke it off because he'd become controlling – to the point of trying to force me out of my mom's house. The breakup didn't end well, but when I threatened the cops on him, he just disappeared."

"Makes sense. He'd already been arrested, so involving the police would have been a bigger issue for Marco."

"But why would he vandalize my store? Or set it on fire, for god sake."

"Look. What we've learned about Marco is disturbing. He hasn't been in a relationship since you. And from what I can see, he started making himself known when you thrust yourself into the limelight. Your store was drawing your attention. Attention, he didn't like." The detective looked at Dawson, "And when you started to hang around her, it only fuelled his obsession."

"Do you know where he is?"

"No – but the recent damage to your truck indicates he's around."

"This is crazy."

"I don't need to tell you how dangerous and unstable a man like him can be. We are confident he set fire to your store. Evidence ties him to the arson. So, you must stay vigilant and let me know if you get any more notes or vandalism. I've already issued a warrant for his arrest, but until he's arrested, you need to be careful."

"Thank you, detective."

Dawson walked him out, locking the door behind him. "I don't know about you, but I need a drink and food. I'll order pizza."

Zoey sat down on the couch, the conversation playing in her head. She never expected a man to obsess over her in a million years. It made no sense.

"I see you brooding over there. Stop. They'll find Marco. This will all be over soon."

"I hope so…"

CHAPTER 23

THE NEXT FEW WEEKS WERE TENSE. ZOEY BOUNCED BETWEEN her mom's and Dawson's house. She felt lost without her store, but the insurance investigator concluded it was not her fault and cut her a check to rebuild. While sitting at Dawson's kitchen table, she searched for a contractor on her computer. He was on shift at the firehouse, leaving her alone to figure things out.

Glancing at the clock, she decided to drive over to the firehouse and surprise him with dinner. She quickly changed into a loose summer dress and pulled her hair into a messy bun.

Grabbing her phone, she texted her mom that she'd swing by on her way back from seeing Dawson. After stopping to grab some Chinese, she parked her car and hurried into the station.

"Hello!" she called out, "I brought dinner!"

Captain Pountz popped out to greet her, "Zoey! How are you? Here, let me help you." He grabbed the big box she was balancing on her hip. "Come on inside… everyone will be glad to see you."

Since she'd been unemployed, she'd used much of her free time bringing snacks and goodies to Dawson's shift at the station. They treated her as part of the family whenever she was there.

"Dawson! I found something that belongs to you…" Captain called out. Kristof and Oren barreled into the dining room, laughing and cutting up.

"Zoey!" they smashed her in a group hug.

"Hey, fuckers, off my woman." Dawson pulled her from their grip and kissed her. "This is a nice surprise."

"I missed you and thought you'd like some dinner."

"You didn't need to bring me dinner to visit."

"Speak for yourself, Dawson. I am always happy when your woman shows up with food… she keeps us fed well!" Lt. Hill laughed.

Just as Corey Davis, the EMT on shift, strolled into the room, the alarm bell went off.

"Well, fuck," Dawson frowned.

Station Three – all units. Signal 33 structure fire.

1701 Cape Boulevard

"That's my mom's," Zoey gasped, digging her phone out of her bag. Her call went straight to voicemail.

"She's not answering. Oh God, Dawson…"

Dawson kissed her, "Let's go, guys. Zoey, don't leave the station. Please."

She watched as the trucks tore out of the station. Zoey didn't wait. She ran to her car and tore out behind them. There was no way she was waiting at the station when her mom wasn't answering her phone.

———

DAWSON'S LEG bounced nervously as the truck sped down the road.

"Hey man, you ok?"

"Let's just get there."

Uri nodded, "Her mom is going to be fine."

As they pulled onto her street, Dawson noticed there was no sign of fire. No smoke. Nothing.

"The neighbor who called it in said they thought they saw smoke coming from the backside. But I do not see anything, you?"

Dawson bolted out of the truck.

"There," he pointed to a tiny wisp of grey billowing up from the rear of her house. He ran toward the side, coming to an immediate halt, when he found Zoey's mother pointing a shotgun toward a man.

"Katrina?"

"Oh, Dawson. This moron tried to start a fire in my backyard. I caught him dousing my bushes in lighter fluid."

"Um… ok."

"He wasn't expecting a little old lady to pull a gun on him. Idiot."

She set the gun down against the house as Dawson leaned down and grabbed the man's neck. Lifting him, he twisted his arm and walked him towards the front.

"Whoa… what the hell?" Lt. Hill glanced at the man in Dawson's grasp.

"This fucker tried to set her house on fire. Go around the back and hose down the backside. He poured lighter fluid everywhere. Ms. Horton subdued him before he could set this place ablaze."

"DAWSON!" Zoey flung herself out of her car. "Where's my mom…. YOU!" She skidded to a halt, "Why, MARCO?" She spat in his face.

"You were mine."

"So, you tried to set me on fire? My mom on fire? What the fuck is wrong with you?"

Her mother walked around the house, holding onto Lt. Hill. "ZOEY!"

Zoey ran towards her mother and embraced her, "Thank god. When I heard the call, I freaked out."

"I'm fine. He wasn't expecting a gun-toting old woman."

Police arrived and arrested Marco. Dawson hugged her tight as they watched them drive away with him in the back of a squad car.

"Well… we have enough to put Marco away for a long time, Miss Horton." The detective shook Dawson's hand and gave her a soft hug.

"Thank you."

Zoey smiled as the detective left, turning towards Dawson, "I think I'll stay here with my mom. Y'all enjoy the food. You should be able to heat it up."

"Seriously… you're worried about us and dinner?" Dawson kissed her cheek, "Take care of your mom tonight. I'll be here for breakfast in the morning."

"Sounds good." She kissed him hard on the lips, "I love you."

"I love you."

Dawson climbed into the truck, relieved the call went how it had. He wasn't sure how he'd have handled it if something had happened to her mother. He was all too familiar with what losing a parent to a sudden tragedy was like. She'd never feel that loss if he had his way.

As the truck pulled off the curb, his eyes followed her into the house.

Zoey and her mom stayed up talking about the events that had transpired over the last few weeks. Katrina couldn't stop singing Dawson's praise. She was beyond ecstatic that Zoey had finally met a man who saw her just as she did – beautiful and deserving of love.

Zoey had admitted she was in love with him and that he'd confessed the same for her. Her mom headed towards bed, blabbering about planning a wedding soon. All Zoey could do was smile at her.

After a few exchanged texts and a phone call, Zoey had crashed hard. Her body had been pushed to its limit. After saying goodnight to Dawson, sleep claimed her.

CHAPTER 24

Zoey woke to the sensation of a warm body pressing against her backside. Cracking her eyes open, she glanced over her shoulder and smiled. Dawson was wrapped around her body, sound asleep. Glancing at the clock, she realized it was almost ten in the morning.

Wiggling her body, she pressed her butt into the very awake part of his body. Dawson's arm tightened around her waist, his hand slipping beneath her shirt.

"Morning," Zoey giggled as she looked over her shoulder at him.

"When did you get here?"

"Your mom let me in about forty minutes ago. You looked too cute sleeping; I couldn't resist climbing in bed with you."

Zoey stretched against him, her ass pressing into his aroused state. Dawson kissed her shoulder as he brushed his hand down her side. Zoey inhaled sharply, wiggling as her body reacted to his touch.

"Zoey," Dawson breathed against her skin. "Your ass looks amazing in these shorts." He ran his hand over the barely-there fabric.

Zoey rolled to face him, her hand tracing the lines of his abs. Her hand wound through his hair, pulling his head toward hers as she claimed his lips. Her leg wrapped around him, grinding her aching center against his hardened member.

Zoey moaned as she rocked into him. Dawson responded by tearing off her shorts, ripping them at the seam.

"I'll buy you a new pair… but I need to be buried inside you now." Dawson kicked off his boxers and straddled her body. He nipped and sucked down her neck, licking a trail towards her hardened nipples. He pulled the tiny bud into her mouth as he pushed his cock inside her warm pussy.

Zoey hissed, thrusting her hips and arching her back into his body. "FUCK," she moaned out. Her eyes rolled into the back of her head as he started to pump in and out of her.

"I love the way your warm pussy wraps around my cock," Dawson grunted as he buried himself deeper, "you make me want to fill you with my cum." He pressed his lips to hers.

Zoey couldn't stop herself from screaming out, "Fuck… Dawson… right there! Please harder. OH GOD…I'm going to…"

Dawson pounded his dick into her faster. He could feel her clenching his cock, her walls tightening around him.

"That's it, baby. I want to feel your juices coat my cock. Let go and cum."

"OH, GOD!" Zoey screamed. Her pussy spasmed, milking his shaft for all he had. Dawson kept driving himself inside her. Closing his eyes and giving in to the sensation of her body as he rode out her orgasm.

Grabbing her hips, Dawson flipped them over, never slipping out of her, and settled her on top of him.

"You make my cock so hard, Zoey." He fisted her hair, tugging her down to claim her lips. "Ride my cock, baby." He gripped her waist as she sat up and started to rock.

"Goddamn," Dawson moaned, "That's it, baby. Fuck my dick like you mean it."

Zoey bounced and writhed against his rigid member. Her whole body rocked in rhythm with his.

"Dawson," she cried, "I'm so close."

"Don't stop, Zoey." Dawson pushed her hips, pressing his cock deeper.

"Cum with me. Please…" Zoey sped up, "I want to feel your cock pulsating inside me."

Dawson lost all sense of control as his movements became frantic. He raced towards his release. He grunted, feeling his balls tighten.

"Zoey…" he pleaded. His release was close. His finger traced her leg, pressing down on her tiny nub of nerves. It was all that she needed to lose control.

He knew the moment she fell over the edge. Her womb locked down on his cock, squeezing it like a vice grip. Dawson swore he saw stars as his cock exploded inside her.

"FUCK!"

He pumped his dick into her cunt, his seed spilling deep inside her. His cum leaked out, mixing with her juices as the remnants of their lovemaking dripped down his shaft.

Zoey collapsed on his chest, her breaths coming out in shallow pants.

Dawson wrapped his arms around her, shifting them to face each other in the bed. His semi-erect cock slipped from her warm center.

"That was…" Zoey pressed a kiss to his chest, "Amazing."

"I love you, Zoey."

"And I love you. But," She propped herself onto her elbow, "as much as I'd like to stay wrapped up in your arms, I'm starving."

Dawson chuckled, "How about a shower, then breakfast."

Dawson helped her from the bed and followed her into her tiny bathroom.

They slipped on some clothes after another round of love-making under the warm water. Dawson slipped his hand in hers as they left the room. All he could think about was making her his forever, but he knew she wasn't ready despite being in love with him.

CHAPTER 25

Weeks turned into a month, and Zoey was getting stir-crazy. Living with her mother wasn't horrible; it wasn't what she wanted. The insurance adjusters had finally come to a settlement and paid out her fire claim. Unfortunately, there was nothing left of the tiny shop. She was going to have to rebuild from scratch.

Zoey was grateful the fire department had spared the nearby stores. They'd only suffered minimal damage from smoke and water. But in a few weeks, they would be back open for business—while her place remained closed.

Dawson was as attentive as ever. They saw each other every day unless he was at the firehouse. Even then, they texted or FaceTimed each other.

Zoey smiled, thinking about their call this morning. Dawson was at the station, and he'd called and woken her up with a serenade. Every day, she learned something new about him – like how he had a sexy voice to match his rocking body. The crew had been in the background, singing right along with him. Her mind drifted off, recalling the way he sounded as he sang.

"Good morning, baby."

Dawson's smile filled her screen as she stretched on her bed. "Hey, you." Zoey sat up. She noticed the team in the background. "Hey, Guys."

Zoey could hear the soft music playing in the truck bay. "What are you guys doing? It's only," she glanced at the clock, "eight-thirty in the morning."

"We're washing the rig. Ignore them… they're messing around."

"Don't listen to him, Zoey!" Uri screamed in the background. "This fool has been singing sappy love songs all morning— making us sick!"

"I didn't know you could sing." Zoey smiled.

"Nah… just along with the radio."

"Sing something for me," Zoey pouted, "Please…"

Dawson turned around and said something to Uri. Uri gave him a thumbs-up, and Zoey watched as he fiddled with his phone. Zoey gasped when she heard the music start. Glancing at Dawson, she nearly fell off the bed when he broke into Jason Mraz, I'm Yours.

This, oh this, this is our fate, I'm yours…

She lost herself in the hypnotic tone of his voice. It wasn't until Uri's soft chuckle in the background that she snapped out of her trance.

"Holy shit, Dawson..." Zoey struggled for words. "I didn't know you could sing like that—I mean, is there anything you can't do?"

"Yeah—hold you right now." The alarm sounded in the background. "Sorry, babe. Gotta run. Stop by later. I love you."

"Love you, too." Zoey set the phone down, stunned. He amazed her every day they were together.

Snapping from her memory, she stared at the charred building before her. She was meeting the contractor to discuss her options moving forward. She sucked in a deep breath and waited. Her whole life had gone up in flames, yet, standing there, she felt happier than she had in years.

CHAPTER 26

Dawson stood off to the side, watching Zoey. He'd convinced the guys to swing by her shop on the way back from their last call. Now, parked on the curb, he stared at her in a trance.

"You just going to stare at her, or are you going to go and give her a morning kiss?" Uri joked from behind the steering wheel.

Dawson smiled, "Yeah… I'll be right back."

He slipped from the truck, slowly approaching her on the sidewalk. Slipping up behind her, he wrapped his arms around her midsection.

Zoey jumped as he pressed his lips to the tender flesh where her neck met her shoulder.

"It's me." His hot breath whispered into her ear.

"I hope so," Zoey giggled as she spun in his arms, "Or a stranger is about to get kneed in the balls." She pressed her lips to his.

"I needed to see you, so I convinced the guys to swing by."

Zoey peered over his shoulder, spotting the giant red truck on the street. She threw her hand up in a wave at his teammates, watching them from inside the rig.

"Well… tell them thank you."

"The builder running late?"

"Looks that way." Zoey let out a frustrated sigh.

"Hey… don't stress. I promise it will all work out."

"I know. It's just…" Zoey took a breath, "this wasn't in my plan. You know. I have to start all over again. It's so frustrating."

"Well, this time, you're not alone. You have me."

"Thank you." Zoey kissed him again, "Have I told you I love you lately?"

"Yes, but I never get tired of hearing it."

Dawson's radio beeped. The sound of dispatch filled the air, reminding them he was at work.

"Shit – I gotta go. Call me, let me know what he says."

"I will. Be careful – I'll try to stop by."

Zoey watched as he got in the truck and pulled off.

"Excuse me," a voice caused her to jump. "Sorry, I didn't mean to startle you. Are you Zoey Horton?"

"Yes," Zoey smiled, "I take it you're the contractor?"

"Yeah – Mike Prince," he shook her hand, "shall we get started?"

Zoey followed him into the wreckage and listened as he talked about his recommendations. He suggested turning the second floor into an open loft for her work portions of the shop and the lower level for sales. He also thought moving the office upstairs was a better option. Zoey liked the idea but told him she'd have to think it over since this had been her living space before the fire. She'd have to keep living with her mother if she took his recommendation. She wasn't sure if she wanted to commit to that just yet.

WHEN ZOEY WALKED IN, Dawson was sitting on the couch in the common area. He could tell she was stressed about something right away.

"What's wrong? Did your meeting not go well?"

Zoey smiled as she sat beside him, "It went well. I need to decide whether or not I want to make the changes he's suggesting."

Dawson wrapped his arm around her, "What did he recommend?"

Zoey spent the next few minutes going over the contractor's plans.

"So… I have to decide if I can stand living with my mom or not."

"Or…" Dawson swallowed, "you could just move in with me."

"What?" Zoey lifted her head to look at him, "are you asking me to move in with you?"

"I don't see why not. We're always together anyway."

"I don't want you to offer out of some sense of nobility or something."

"Are you serious, Zoey?" Dawson shifted, "I love you. I wouldn't have asked for any other reason other than that."

Zoey appraised him, "Thank you." She pressed her lips to his, "I still don't know what I did to deserve a guy like you, but yes…" she smiled, "I'll move in with you."

"Good. We'll move you in tomorrow when I'm off."

"Wow – that fast?"

"Zoey," he stood, tugging her, "I can't imagine going another moment without you by my side." He pulled her hand, guiding her towards the stairs.

"Where are we going?"

"We're going upstairs."

Several of the guys smirked as Dawson practically dragged Zoey upstairs. Zoey blushed, throwing her hand up in a wave as she stumbled up the steps behind him.

CHAPTER 27

Dawson slammed the door, pressing her body against the wood. His lips scorched her neck as he kissed and nipped at the tender flesh.

"Dawson," Zoey moaned as he rocked his firm erection against her belly.

He lifted her, settling his body between her thighs as she wrapped her legs around his waist. Dawson slipped his hand beneath her dress, sliding his palm against her flesh as he cupped her breast. His lips met hers in a frenzy. Zoey bucked into him.

"Please," she whispered her plea to him.

Dawson slipped her panties to the side and eased his finger between her folds. His touch sent an electric shock to her core. He pumped his digit in and out of her channel as he ground his hardon against her leg.

Zoey couldn't stop the moan from escaping her lips as her orgasm wracked her body. Her womb tightened around his finger; her juices coated his hand as she let go.

Dawson unzipped his pants, setting his cock free. Pushing her panties to the side, he thrust inside her warm pussy. He paused, resting his forehead against hers.

"Everything feels so good with you." Dawson pressed his mouth to hers as he slowly started to pump into her.

"Fuck… Dawson, just like that… oh, God." Zoey moaned, her body contorting as he pounded into her.

"Cum for me, baby. I want to feel you on my cock."

Zoey let go, her belly coiled as her orgasm took control. Dawson grunted, his cock spilling inside her at the same time.

They were both breathless as his hips slowed. Dawson leaned into her body, slowly slipping out of her and setting her on her feet.

"I can't believe we just did that here… I bet your whole department heard us."

"I can't believe I didn't get a call." Dawson waggled his eyebrows at her, eliciting a laugh from Zoey.

"Let me grab you something to clean up with."

Dawson snatched a t-shirt hanging on his bed and kneeled before Zoey. He wiped her legs off and helped her right her dress.

Pressing a kiss to her lips, "Thanks for coming by."

Dawson grabbed his duffle bag off the table next to the door and slipped a key from his key ring, "Here, take this."

"Your key? How will you get inside, though?"

"Zoey – I wasn't kidding when I said I didn't want to be apart from you any longer. Go to my house tonight. I want to come home and crawl in bed with you."

Zoey flushed, "You sure?"

"Yes." The tone sounded, "Shit. Good timing, though." He smiled at her, "Go. I'll call you in a few."

Zoey kissed him goodbye and watched as he hurried down the stairwell. She waited until the firehouse emptied before leaving. Still high from their lovemaking, Zoey navigated the car toward her mom's. She was going to need a few things tonight. She'd get Dawson to help her gather the rest of her stuff tomorrow.

CHAPTER 28

Dawson walked into his house, a slow grin spread across his face when he saw Zoey at the stove cooking breakfast.

"Damn… you're going to spoil me." He stepped behind her and wrapped his arms around her waist.

"I wanted to surprise you," she leaned into his body, pressing her lips to his.

"Smells good."

Zoey finished the pancakes and moved them to the table. Sitting down, she smiled as she shoved a forkful of the buttery goodness in her mouth.

Dawson moaned, "Damn woman, these are fucking amazing."

"So… I thought we could go get my stuff after I meet the contractor."

"I'll go with you to meet him. I need to take a quick shower and change clothes."

"OK. I'll clean up and go get ready myself." Zoey gathered the dishes and dumped them into the sink.

"Or…." Dawson grabbed her and lifted her off the ground, "We can save water and get ready together."

Dawson carried her into the bathroom and set her on her feet. He stripped his shirt off and turned on the water as Zoey peeled her clothes off. Once they were both naked, he laced his fingers with hers and tugged her into the stall.

Grabbing her, he fused their bodies together as he dominated her mouth. His rock-hard cock pressed into her belly as she rocked against him. The warm water cascaded over their skin as their bodies became one. Zoey moaned out in ecstasy as Dawson filled her to the brim. Their bodies moved in tandem. The shower's steam filled the stall as they raced toward their release.

"I can't get enough of you." Dawson pressed his lips to the sensitive spot beneath Zoey's ear.

Zoey flexed her body, her channel clenching around Dawson's thick member. She couldn't stop the pleasure from taking control. Her orgasm burst out of her, every muscle quivering as she screamed out his name. Dawson grunted out, pounding into her pussy as his cum shot out like a dam breaking.

"Fuck…" Dawson eased her down on the ground and steadied himself against the wall. Zoey giggled, pressing a chaste kiss to his chest.

"Zoey… I don't know what I did to deserve you, but damn, I am in love with you." He gathered her into his arms.

"We need to hurry. I'm supposed to meet the contractor soon and give him my answers on renovations."

"Well, let me get you a towel." Dawson cut off the water and hopped out. Grabbing a towel, he wrapped Zoey up and dried himself off. Zoey hurried out of the bathroom, leaving Dawson to stare at his reflection.

He couldn't help but glance into the room Zoey had disappeared into. Dawson knew he didn't want to be apart from Zoey anymore than he had to be. He was unequivocally in love with her.

DAWSON STOOD beside Zoey as she spoke to the contractor. Looking at the remains of her business, he realized how close he'd come to nearly losing her. It made his body shudder.

"Hey," Zoey put her hand on his back. She'd felt him shake, "You alright?" She quirked an eyebrow at him.

"Yeah – sorry. Just realizing I nearly lost you." He tugged her to his side and kissed the top of her head.

"Well, you didn't." She shook hands with the contractor and bid him farewell. "So, what do you think?"

"About what?" Dawson stared at the charred structure.

"The remodel?"

"I think it's going to look great, and I can't wait to see it."

"The contractor seems to think he can finish it in six months."

"Wow, that's quick."

"Yeah—until then, I'm going to ramp up my online sales. I hope you don't mind me turning your spare bedroom into a mini-shop."

"Zoey – it's your house now too."

"I mean, I guess." She blushed.

"I'm serious."

"I know, Dawson… but I'm just your girlfriend. It's still your house."

"Let's fix that then."

"What?" Zoey turned to face him.

"Let's fix that. Make it your house, too."

"You're not making any sense, Dawson."

"Zoey—when I look at this building, I see how close I came to not having you in my life… and that scares me. It makes me realize how fast things can change."

Dawson took her hand, "I want to wake up with you for the rest of my life. I want you to come and see me at work whenever you can. I want to watch you rebuild this business… but most of all, I want you, Zoey. Marry me. Say you'll be mine forever."

Zoey gasped, "Dawson." She watched as he got down on one knee on the sidewalk.

"Please, Zoey. Marry me. Be my wife. Let me love you until the end of time."

"Yes," Zoey's tears spilled down her face as she squatted in front of him. Cradling his face in her hands, she whispered as she pressed her lips to his, "Yes… I love you, Dawson."

They stayed there, half kneeling in one another's embrace on the sidewalk. Dawson finally broke their kiss, "Let's go."

He stood, tugging her up with him.

"Where are we going?"

"To the jeweler. We need to get a ring on that finger so the world knows you're mine."

Dawson practically dragged her down the sidewalk, rushing towards the tiny jewelers on the corner. Zoey couldn't stop laughing as she kept pace with him.

"Slow down, Dawson."

"I can't help it… I want everyone to know how much I love you, Zoey."

Zoey blushed. The reality of her future made her grin stretch across her face. She was going to marry this man. A man who loved her for her—and supported her dreams without question. Zoey tugged his hand, bringing him to a stop outside the shop.

"Dawson," she gripped his hand, "I don't need a ring. I need you."

"I just need you too, baby. But I need a damn ring on your finger so the world knows you're taken. So, let's do this."

He pulled open the door, holding it for Zoey to walk in.

"I love you, Dawson."

"And I love you, Zoey. Let's go start forever."

CHAPTER 29

Zoey couldn't believe today was her wedding day. She and Dawson decided to wait until after her shop was rebuilt. That way, it was one less stressor for them. The contractor had worked double-time, getting the rebuild done in four months.

The shop was doing better than ever. So much better, Zoey had to hire an assistant. She smiled as she watched her mother in the mirror.

"I can't believe my baby is getting married." Katrina dabbed at a stray tear.

"Mom, don't cry because I'll start and mess up my makeup."

"I'm just so proud of you. Your dad would be, too."

Katrina had agreed to walk Zoey down the aisle since her dad died when she was younger. Zoey stood up, straightening her dress. It was a pure white satin gown that hugged her curves. The straps were covered in fabric flowers.

Zoey had opted to forgo the veil, pulling her hair into a simple side twist. Baby's breath was strategically placed in the fold of her twist, giving her a soft look.

She and Dawson had decided to marry on the beach behind her mother's house. Neither of them wanted a big wedding, so the setting was perfect.

"You ready?"

DAWSON STOOD BESIDE CAPTAIN POUNTZ. Shane Pountz was an ordained minister and happily agreed to marry them. Now, waiting at the end of the manmade walkway, Dawson fidgeted nervously in anticipation.

"Stop fidgeting."

"I can't help it." Dawson smiled at his captain. "I want this to hurry up so I can call her my wife."

Shane laughed, "Soon enough, my friend. Soon enough."

The music started, warning him of Zoey's arrival. When Dawson glanced toward the end of the white runner, his breath left his lungs. Her red hair was swept up off her neck, littered with tiny white flowers. Her silken dress hugged her curves, leaving little to his imagination. Dawson shuffled on his feet, trying to hide the massive boner he could feel growing.

She was beautiful.

His eyes followed her as she glided up the walkway towards him. Her mother held her arm as she walked next to Zoey. He could see Katrina fighting back the tears as she escorted her daughter to him.

Dawson couldn't stop smiling. His eyes filled with unleashed tears as Katrina handed Zoey off to him.

Dawson leaned down and kissed Katrina's cheek, "Thank you."

"Take care of my baby, Dawson." Katrina kissed Zoey and took her seat in the front row.

"You look beautiful," Dawson whispered as he gave her a chaste kiss.

"You look pretty good, too." Zoey giggled.

Dawson barely heard Shane's words as he spoke.

"Alright," Shane cleared his throat, "the bride and groom have decided to share their vows. Dawson?" He nodded to Dawson.

"Thanks." Dawson took Zoey's hands in his and faced her.

"Zoey. The first time I saw you was at the Diner. You didn't know it, but I couldn't take my eyes off you. Then, when our station responded to your business on a call – I knew I had to spend more time with you. You refused at first, but I wouldn't take no for an answer. I wanted… no, I needed to make you mine. I know that sounds all caveman, but there was something about you that called out to my soul." Dawson took a deep breath, "Zoey… you lit my world on fire, and the burn I feel for you can only be smoldered with your love. I promise to love you with all of me yesterday, today, and forever."

Zoey shifted on her feet as Dawson slid the custom band on her ring finger. She inhaled and composed herself. Dawson's words struck right to her core.

"Dawson. I've spent my life hiding. Hiding from people… Hiding from myself… Hiding from love.

Then you burst into my life like a match igniting dry land. You make me feel like I'm worthy of love. That I deserve to have someone like you love someone like me.

You've taught me to see myself through your eyes – as a beautiful woman deserving of everything I want and have in life. The air I breathe. The ground I walk on. The life I want means nothing if you're not part of it. I promise to love you with all I am today, tomorrow, forever." Zoey slid the band that matched hers onto his finger.

They laced their hands together, the black and red chrome bands gleaming in the sunlight. Captain Pountz pronounced them husband and wife, but Zoey and Dawson had fused their lips well before his words.

The world disappeared as they held each other close. Finally, taking a breath, Zoey and Dawson realized the crowd had erupted into cheers.

"I love you, Mrs. Ford."

"And I love you, Mr. Ford."

Dawson held Zoey's hand tightly as they took their first steps as husband and wife. The crew from station three witnessed their weddings along with Zoey's mom and her new assistant.

Everyone watched as Dawson and Zoey danced their first dance as a married couple. Dawson held her close, pressing tiny kisses to her neck.

"Do you think they'd be mad if we left?" Dawson whispered into her ear.

"Probably. Let's give it another thirty minutes. Then we can go home, husband."

"Damn, I love the way that sounds on your lips."

"I'm glad because you'll hear it all the time."

"I'll never be sick of hearing it."

"I love you."

Zoey mashed her lips to his, kissing him like no one was watching. Her heart was ready to combust with love and desire.

"You know what… let's bail. I don't care if they get mad." Zoey tugged his hand, leading him off the dance floor.

After bidding farewell to everyone, Zoey and Dawson hurried towards his truck.

"You ready to start forever?" Dawson put the truck in drive.

"Are you ready?" Zoey smirked, pursing her lips at him.

"Baby… I was born ready."

Zoey pinched herself. She still couldn't believe she was married to the man beside her. She felt she wasn't worthy of a love like this all her life. Dawson knocked down all her barriers and set her soul on fire.

They pulled into their driveway. Dawson killed the engine, "Wait there." He jumped out of the truck and ran around to Zoey's side.

"Dawson, what are you doing?" Zoey smiled at her husband, standing in her doorway.

"I'm going to carry my wife into our house." Dawson pulled her from the seat and cradled her into his arms.

"Dawson," Zoey giggled.

"Zoey, I won't get another chance to carry my wife over the threshold for the first time. Indulge me."

Zoey nestled her face into the crook of his neck as he carried her through the door. Dawson kicked it shut as Zoey whispered, "I love you, Dawson."

"I love you, Zoey. Now – let's start forever together."

EPILOGUE

Davey watched his co-worker pull out of the driveway and head off to start his life with his new wife. He was happy Dawson got what he wanted—he knew what loss felt like.

Chief Donnelly's hand dropped on his shoulder, making him turn. "Hey, Chief."

"Davey… it was a good day today." He smiled as his wife leaned against him. "It's nice when we add new members to station six's family."

Davey quirked a brow, knowing he was referring to him too. "Yeah… Zoey is one hell of a woman."

"You could have that." He arched his brow at him, making Jason snort.

"Nope. Not for me, Chief." Davey wasn't brave like Dawson. He was happy keeping things casual because no commitments meant no heartbreak. "I live for the job. You never know." Davey elbowed Donnelly in the gut. "One day, I'm gonna swoop in and take your job."

"I'll gladly give it to you. This woman deserves to get my last years all to herself." He pressed a kiss to his wife's head. "Who will you spend your last years on this earth with if you never open up for someone?"

"I tried that once, sir. Didn't work out for me, so I think I'll get a dog instead." Davey laughed, walking toward his truck.

"I can't wait for the day you have to eat your words, son." Donnelly shook his head. "Because there's going to be a woman who comes into your life, and you're going to realize her happiness is more important than any memory you still hold on to."

Davey watched as his Chief turned and walked his wife to their car. He drew in a deep breath and sighed. He was wrong. He was just fine being alone. It would take something big for a woman to wreck the walls around his heart—because that's the only way he would ever fall in love.

Want to know if Davey meets the woman who finally crashes through the barrier around his heart?

Find out in Signal 63: Reviving London, Available HERE

ALSO BY LC TAYLOR

Simply scan the QR code to find your next great read.

Can't scan?

No worries... simply visit

www.behindthebadgepress.com

ABOUT LC

"Grab me a shot of whiskey. These books are about tattooed men and guns!"

What can I say? I'm a down home southern girl who bleeds red, white, and blue, so welcome to My world. I'm an International and USA Today best-selling author, who's an unapologetic down-home southern gal, with a bit of a dirty mouth.

But… I've never met a brooding hero I didn't love. I write my men cut, tattooed and tender, for their down, but-not-out ladies, who just need a little love from the right man.

When I'm not writing my Crossroads Heroes series, creating swoon-worthy love connections, or indulging my darker desires as my alter ego Dori P, I'm curled up with a glass of peach crown and my very own sexy tattooed cop on the couch watching reruns of Chicago Fire..

www.ingramcontent.com/pod-product-compliance
Lightning Source LLC
Chambersburg PA
CBHW060331310726
48976CB00007B/2527